Risen from the Ranks

Or, Harry Walton's Success

Horatio Alger, Jr.

PREFACE

"Risen from the Ranks" contains the further history of Harry Walton, who was first introduced to the public in the pages of "Bound to Rise." Those who are interested in learning how far he made good the promise of his boyhood, may here find their curiosity gratified. For the benefit of those who may only read the present volume, a synopsis of Harry's previous life is given in the first chapter.

In describing Harry's rise from the ranks I have studiously avoided the extraordinary incidents and pieces of good luck, which the story writer has always at command, being desirous of presenting my hero's career as one which may be imitated by the thousands of boys similarly placed, who, like him, are anxious to rise from the ranks. It is my hope that this story, suggested in part by the career of an eminent American editor, may afford encouragement to such boys, and teach them that "where there is a will there is always a way."

New York, October 1874.

CHAPTER I.

HARRY WALTON.

"I am sorry to part with you, Harry," said Professor Henderson. "You have been a very satisfactory and efficient assistant, and I shall miss you."

"Thank you, sir," said Harry. "I have tried to be faithful to your interests."

"You have been so," said the Professor emphatically. "I have had perfect confidence in you, and this has relieved me of a great deal of anxiety. It would have been very easy for one in your position to cheat me out of a considerable sum of money."

"It was no credit to me to resist such a temptation as that," said Harry.

"I am glad to hear you say so, but it shows your inexperience nevertheless. Money is the great tempter nowadays. Consider how many defalcations and breaches of trust we read of daily in confidential positions, and we are forced to conclude that honesty is a rarer virtue than we like to think it. I have every reason to believe that my assistant last winter purloined, at the least, a hundred dollars, but I was unable to prove it, and submitted to the loss. It may be the same next winter. Can't I induce you to change your resolution, and remain in my employ? I will advance your pay."

"Thank you, Professor Henderson," said Harry gratefully. "I appreciate your offer, even if I do not accept it. But I have made up mind to learn the printing business."

"You are to enter the office of the 'Centreville Gazette,' I believe."

"Yes, sir."

"How much pay will you get?"

"I shall receive my board the first month, and for the next six months have agreed to take two dollars a week and board."

"That won't pay your expenses."

"It must," said Harry, firmly.

"You have laid up some money while with me, haven't you!"

"Yes, sir; I have fifty dollars in my pocket-book, besides having given eighty dollars at home."

"That is doing well, but you won't be able to lay up anything for the next year."

"Perhaps not in money, but I shall be gaining the knowledge of a good trade."

"And you like that better than remaining with me, and learning my business?"

"Yes, sir."

"Well, perhaps you are right. I don't fancy being a magician myself; but I am too old to change. I like moving round, and I make a good living for my family. Besides I contribute to the innocent amusement of the public, and earn my money fairly."

"I agree with you, sir," said Harry. "I think yours is a useful employment, but it would not suit everybody. Ever since I read the life of Benjamin Franklin, I have wanted to learn to be a printer."

"It is an excellent business, no doubt, and if you have made up your mind I will not dissuade you. When you have a paper of your own, you can give your old friend, Professor Henderson, an occasional puff."

"I shall be glad to do that," said Harry, smiling, "but I shall have to wait some time first."

"How old are you now?"

"Sixteen."

"Then you may qualify yourself for an editor in five or six years. I advise you to try it at any rate. The editor in America is a man of influence."

"I do look forward to it," said Harry, seriously. "I should not be satisfied to remain a journeyman all my life, nor even the half of it."

"I sympathize with your ambition, Harry," said the Professor, earnestly, "and I wish you the best success. Let me hear from you occasionally."

"I should be very glad to write you, sir."

"I see the stage is at the door, and I must bid you good-by. When you have a vacation, if you get a chance to come our way, Mrs. Henderson and myself will be glad to receive a visit from you. Good-by!" And with a hearty shake of the hand, Professor Henderson bade farewell to his late assistant.

Those who have read "Bound to Rise," and are thus familiar with Harry Walton's early history, will need no explanation of the preceding conversation. But for the benefit of new readers, I will recapitulate briefly the leading events in the history of the boy of sixteen who is to be our hero.

Harry Walton was the oldest son of a poor New Hampshire farmer, who found great difficulty is wresting from his few sterile acres a living for his family. Nearly a year before, he had lost his only cow by a prevalent disease, and being without money, was compelled to buy another of Squire Green, a rich but mean neighbor, on a six months' note, on very unfavorable terms. As it required great economy to make both ends meet, there seemed no possible chance of his being able to meet the note at maturity. Beside, Mr. Walton was to forfeit ten dollars if he did not have the principal and interest ready for Squire Green. The hard-hearted creditor was mean enough to take advantage of his poor neighbor's necessities, and there was not the slightest chance of his receding from his unreasonable demand. Under these circumstances Harry, the oldest boy, asked his father's permission to go out into the world and earn his own living. He hoped not only to do this, but to save something toward paying his father's note. His ambition had been kindled by reading the life of Benjamin Franklin, which had been awarded to him as a school prize. He did not expect to emulate Franklin, but he thought that by imitating him he might attain an honorable position in the community.

Harry's request was not at first favorably received. To send a boy out into the world to earn his own living is a hazardous experiment, and fathers are less sanguine than their sons. Their experience suggests difficulties and obstacles of which the inexperienced youth knows and possesses nothing. But in the present case Mr. Walton reflected that the little farming town in which he lived offered small inducements for a boy to remain there, unless he was content to be a farmer, and this required capital. His farm was too small for himself, and of course he could not give Harry a part when be came of age. On the whole, therefore, Harry's plan of becoming a mechanic seemed not so bad a one after all. So permission was accorded, and our hero, with his little bundle of clothes, left the paternal roof, and went out in quest of employment.

After some adventures Harry obtained employment in a shoe-shop as pegger. A few weeks sufficed to make him a good workman, and he was then able to earn three dollars a week and board. Out of this sum be hoped to save enough to pay the note held by Squire Green against his father, but there were two unforeseen obstacles. He had the misfortune to lose his pocket-book, which was picked up by an unprincipled young man, by name Luke Harrison, also a shoemaker, who was always in pecuniary difficulties, though he earned much higher wages than Harry. Luke was unable to resist the temptation, and appropriated the money to his own use. This Harry ascertained after a while, but thus far had succeeded in obtaining the restitution of but a small portion of his hard-earned savings. The second obstacle was a sudden depression in the shoe trade which threw him out of work. More than most occupations the shoe business is liable to these sudden fluctuations and suspensions, and the most industrious and ambitious workman is often compelled to spend in his enforced weeks of idleness all that he had been able to save when employed, and thus at the end of the year finds himself, through no fault of his own, no better off than at the beginning. Finding himself out of work, our hero visited other shoe establishments in the hope of employment. But his search was in vain. Chance in this emergency made him acquainted with Professor Henderson, a well-known magician and conjurer, whose custom it was to travel, through the fall and winter, from town to town, giving public exhibitions of his skill. He was in want of an assistant, to sell tickets and help him generally, and he offered the position to our hero, at a salary of five dollars a week. It is needless to say that the position was gladly accepted. It was not the business that Harry preferred, but he reasoned justly that it was honorable, and was far better than remaining idle. He found Professor Henderson as he called himself, a considerate and agreeable employer, and as may be inferred from the conversation with which this chapter begins, his services were very satisfactory. At the close of the six months, he had the satisfaction of paying the note which his father had given, and so of disappointing the selfish schemes of the grasping creditor.

This was not all. He met with an adventure while travelling for the Professor, in which a highwayman who undertook to rob him, came off second best, and he was thus enabled to add fifty dollars to his savings. His financial condition at the opening of the present story has already been set forth.

Though I have necessarily omitted many interesting details, to be found in "Bound to Rise," I have given the reader all the information required to enable him to understand the narrative of Harry's subsequent fortunes.

CHAPTER 11.

THE PRINTING OFFICE.

Jotham Anderson, editor and publisher of the "Centreville Gazette," was sitting at his desk penning an editorial paragraph, when the office door opened, and Harry Walton entered.

"Good-morning, Mr. Anderson," said our hero, removing his hat.

"Good-morning, my friend. I believe you have the advantage of me," replied the editor.

Our hero was taken aback. It didn't occur to him that the engagement was a far less important event to the publisher than to himself. He began to be afraid that the place had not been kept open for him.

"My name is Harry Walton," he explained. "I was travelling with Prof. Henderson last winter, and called here to get some bills printed."

"Oh yes, I remember you now. I agreed to take you into the office," said the editor, to Harry's great relief.

"Yes, air."

"You haven't changed your mind, then?—You still want to be a printer?"

"Yes, sir."

"You have left the Professor, I suppose."

"I left him yesterday."

"What did he pay you?"

"Five dollars a week. He offered me six, if I would stay with him."

"Of course you know that I can't pay you any such wages at present."

"Yes, sir. You agreed to give me my board the first month, and two dollars a week for six months afterward."

"That is all you will be worth to me at first. It is a good deal less than you would earn with Professor Henderson."

"I know that, sir; but I am willing to come for that."

"Good. I see you are in earnest about printing, and that is a good sign. I wanted you to understand just what you had to expect, so that you need not be disappointed."

"I sha'n't be disappointed, sir," said Harry confidently. "I have made up my mind to be a printer, and if you didn't receive me into your office, I would try to get in somewhere else."

"Then no more need be said. When do you want to begin?"

"I am ready any time."

"Where is your trunk?"

"At the tavern."

"You can have it brought over to my house whenever you please. The hotel-keeper will send it over for you. He is our expressman. Come into the house now, and I will introduce you to my wife."

The editor's home was just across the street from his printing office. Followed by Harry he crossed the street, opened the front door, and led the way into the sitting-room, where a pleasant-looking lady of middle age was seated.

"My dear," he said, "I bring you a new boarder."

She looked at Harry inquiringly.

"This young man," her husband explained, "is going into the office to learn printing. I have taken a contract to make a second Benjamin Franklin of him."

"Then you'll do more for him than you have been able to do for yourself," said Mrs. Anderson, smiling.

"You are inclined to be severe, Mrs. Anderson, but I fear you are correct. However, I can be like a guide-post, which points the way which it does not travel. Can you show Harry Walton—for that is his name—where you propose to put him?"

"I am afraid I must give you a room in the attic," said Mrs. Anderson. "Our house is small, and all the chambers on the second floor are occupied."

"I am not at all particular," said Harry. "I have not been accustomed to elegant accommodations."

"If you will follow me upstairs, I will show you your room."

Pausing on the third landing, Mrs. Anderson found the door of a small but comfortable bed-room. There was no carpet on the floor, but it was painted yellow, and scrupulously clean. A bed, two chairs, a bureau and wash-stand completed the list of furniture.

"I shall like this room very well," said our hero.

"There is a closet," said the lady, pointing to a door in the corner. "It is large enough to contain your trunk, if you choose to put it in there. I hope you don't smoke."

"Oh, no, indeed," said Harry, laughing. "I haven't got so far along as that."

"Mr. Anderson's last apprentice—he is a journeyman now—was a smoker. He not only scented up the room, but as he was very careless about lights, I was continually alarmed lest he should set the house on fire. Finally, I got so nervous that I asked him to board somewhere else."

"Is he working for Mr. Anderson now?"

"Yes; you probably saw him in the office."

"I saw two young men at the case."

"The one I speak of is the youngest. His name is John Clapp."

"There is no danger of my smoking. I don't think it would do me any good. Besides, it is expensive, and I can't afford it."

"I see we think alike," said Mrs. Anderson, smiling. "I am sure we will get along well together."

"I shall try not to give you any trouble," said our hero, and his tone, which was evidently sincere, impressed Mrs. Anderson still more favorably.

"You won't find me very hard to suit, I hope. I suppose you will be here to supper?"

"If it will he quite convenient. My trunk is at the tavern, and I could stay there till morning, if you wished."

"Oh, no, come at once. Take possession of the room now, if you like, and leave an order to have your trunk brought here."

"Thank you. What is your hour for supper?"

"Half-past five."

"Thank you. I will go over and speak to Mr. Anderson a minute."

The editor looked up as Harry reappeared.

"Well, have you settled arrangements with Mrs. Anderson?" he asked.

"Yes, sir, I believe so."

"I hope you like your room."

"It is very comfortable. It won't take me long to feel at home there."

"Did she ask you whether you smoked?"

"Yes, sir."

"I thought she would. That's where Clapp and she fell out."

Harry's attention was drawn to a thin, sallow young man of about twenty, who stood at a case on the opposite side of the room.

"Mrs. Anderson was afraid I would set the house on fire," said the young man thus referred to.

"Yes, she felt nervous about it. However, it is not surprising. An uncle of hers lost his house in that way. I suppose you don't smoke, Walton?"

"No, sir."

"Clapp smokes for his health. You see how stout and robust he is," said the editor, a little satirically.

"It doesn't do me any harm," said Clapp, a little testily.

"Oh, well, I don't interfere with you, though I think you would be better off if you should give up the habit. Ferguson don't smoke."

This was the other compositor, a man of thirty, whose case was not far distant from Clapp's.

"I can't afford it," said Ferguson; "nor could Clapp, if he had a wife and two young children to support."

"Smoking doesn't cost much," said the younger journeyman.

"So you think; but did you ever reckon it up?"

"No."

"Don't you keep any accounts?"

"No; I spend when I need to, and I can always tell how much I have left. What's the use of keeping accounts?"

"You can tell how you stand."

"I can tell that without taking so much trouble."

"You see we must all agree to disagree," said Mr. Anderson. "I am afraid Clapp isn't going to be a second Benjamin Franklin."

"Who is?" asked Clapp.

"Our young friend here," said the editor.

"Oh, is he?" queried the other with a sneer. "It'll be a great honor
I'm sure, to have him in the office."
"Come, no chaffing, Clapp," said Mr. Anderson.

Harry hastened to disclaim the charge, for Clapp's sneer affected him disagreeably.

"I admire Franklin," he said, "but there isn't much danger of my turning out a second edition of him."

"Professional already, I see, Walton," said the editor.

"When shall I go to work, Mr. Anderson?"

"Whenever you are ready."

"I am ready now."

"You are prompt."

"You won't be in such a hurry to go to work a week hence," said Clapp.

"I think I shall," said Harry. "I am anxious to learn as fast as possible."

"Oh, I forgot. You want to become a second Franklin."

"I sha'n't like him," thought our hero. "He seems to try to make himself disagreeable."

"Mr. Ferguson will give you some instruction, and set you to work," said his employer.

Harry was glad that it was from the older journeyman that he was to receive his first lesson, and not from the younger.

CHAPTER III.

HARRY STUMBLES UPON AN ACQUAINTANCE.

After supper Harry went round to the tavern to see about his trunk. A group of young men were in the bar-room, some of whom looked up as he entered. Among these was Luke Harrison, who was surprised and by no means pleased to see his creditor. Harry recognized him at the same instant, and said, "How are you, Luke?"

"Is that you, Walton?" said Luke. "What brings you to Centreville?
Professor Henderson isn't here, is he?"
"No; I have left him."

"Oh, you're out of a job, are you?" asked Luke, in a tone of satisfaction, for we are apt to dislike those whom we have injured, and for this reason he felt by no means friendly.

"No, I'm not," said Harry, quietly. "I've found work in Centreville."

"Gone back to pegging, have you? Whose shop are you in?"

"I am in a different business."

"You don't say! What is it?" asked Luke, with some curiosity.

"I'm in the office of the 'Centreville Gazette.' I'm going to learn the printing business."

"You are? Why, I've got a friend in the office,—John Clapp. He never told me about your being there."

"He didn't know I was coming. I only went to work this afternoon."

"So you are the printer's devil?" said Luke, with a slight sneer.

"I believe so," answered our hero, quietly.

"Do you get good pay?"

"Not much at first. However, I can get along with what money I have, and what is due me."

Luke Harrison understood the last allusion, and turned away abruptly. He had no wish to pay up the money which he owed Harry, and for this reason was sorry to see him in the village. He feared, if the conversation were continued, Harry would be asking for the money, and this would be disagreeable.

At this moment John Clapp entered the bar-room. He nodded slightly to Harry, but walked up to Luke, and greeted him cordially. There were many points of resemblance between them, and this drew them into habits of intimacy.

"Will you have something to drink, Harrison?" said Clapp.

"I don't mind if I do," answered Luke, with alacrity.

They walked up to the bar, and they were soon pledging each other in a fiery fluid which was not very likely to benefit either of them. Meanwhile Harry gave directions about his trunk, and left the room.

"So you've got a new 'devil' in your office," said Luke, after draining his glass.

"Yes. He came this afternoon. How did you hear?"

"He told me."

"Do you know him?" asked Clapp, in some surprise.

"Yes. I know him as well as I want to."

"What sort of a fellow is he?"

"Oh, he's a sneak—one of your pious chaps, that 'wants to be an angel, and with the angels stand.'"

"Then he's made a mistake in turning 'devil,'" said Clapp.

"Good for you!" said Luke, laughing. "You're unusually brilliant to-night, Clapp."

"So he's a saint, is he?"

"He set up for one; but I don't like his style myself. He's as mean as dirt. Why I knew him several months, and he never offered to treat in all that time. He's as much afraid of spending a cent as if it were a dollar."

"He won't have many dollars to spend just at present. He's working for his board."

"Oh, he's got money saved up," said Luke. "Fellows like him hang on to a cent when they get it. I once asked him to lend me a few dollars, just for a day or two, but he wouldn't do it. I hate such mean fellows."

"So do I. Will you have a cigar?"

"I'll treat this time," said Luke, who thought it polite to take his turn in treating once to his companion's four or five times.

"Thank you. From what you say, I am sorry Anderson has taken the fellow into the office."

"You needn't have much to say to him."

"I shan't trouble myself much about him. I didn't like his looks when I first set eyes on him. I suppose old Mother Anderson will like him. She couldn't abide my smoking, and he won't trouble her that way."

"So; he's too mean to buy the cigars."

"He said he couldn't afford it."

"That's what it comes to. By the way, Clapp, when shall we take another ride?"

"I can get away nest Monday afternoon, at three."

"All right. I'll manage to get off at the same time. We'll go to Whiston and take supper at the hotel. It does a fellow good to get off now and then. It won't cost more than five dollars apiece altogether."

"We'll get the carriage charged. The fact is, I'm little low on funds."

"So am I, but it won't matter. Griffin will wait for his pay."

While Harry's character waa being so unfavorably discussed, he was taking a walk by himself, observing with interest the main features of his new home. He had been here before with Professor Henderson, but had been too much occupied at that time to get a very clear idea of Centreville, nor had it then the interest for him which it had acquired since. He went upon a hill overlooking the village, and obtained an excellent view from its summit. It was a pleasant, well-built village of perhaps three thousand inhabitants, with outlying farms and farm-houses. Along the principal streets the dwellings and stores were closely built, so as to make it seem quite city-like. It was the shire town of the county, and being the largest place in the neighborhood, country people for miles around traded at its stores. Farmers' wives came to Centreville to make purchases, just as ladies living within a radius of thirty miles visit New York and Boston, for a similar purpose. Altogether, therefore, Centreville was quite a lively place, and a town of considerable local importance. The fact that it had a weekly paper of its own, contributed to bring it into notice. Nor was that all. Situated on a little hillock was a building with a belfry, which might have been taken for a church but for a play-ground near by, which indicated that it had a different character. It was in fact the Prescott Academy, so called from the name of its founder, who had endowed it with a fund of ten thousand dollars, besides erecting the building at his own expense on land bought for the purpose. This academy also had a local reputation, and its benefits were not confined to the children of Centreville. There were about twenty pupils from other towns who boarded with the Principal or elsewhere in the town, and made up the whole number of students in attendance—about eighty on an average.

Standing on the eminence referred to, Harry's attention was drawn to the Academy, and he could not help forming the wish that he, too, might share in its advantages.

"There is so much to learn, and I know so little," he thought.

But he did not brood over the poverty which prevented him from gratifying his desire. He knew it would do no good, and he also reflected that knowledge may be acquired in a printing office as well as within the walls of an academy or college.

"As soon as I get well settled," he said to himself, "I mean to get some books and study a little every day. That is the way Franklin did. I never can be an editor, that's certain, without knowing more than I do now. Before I am qualified to teach others, I must know something myself."

Looking at the village which lay below him, Harry was disposed to congratulate himself on his new residence.

"It looks like a pleasant place," he said to himself, "and when I get a little acquainted, I shall enjoy myself very well, I am sure. Of course I shall feel rather lonely just at first."

He was so engrossed by his thoughts that he did not take heed to his steps, and was only reminded of his abstraction by his foot suddenly coming in contact with a boy who was lying under a tree, and pitching headfirst over him.

"Holloa!" exclaimed the latter, "what are you about? You didn't take me for a foot-ball, did you?"

"I beg your pardon," said Harry, jumping up in some confusion. "I was so busy thinking that I didn't see you. I hope I didn't hurt you."

"Nothing serious. Didn't you hurt yourself?"

"I bumped my head a little, but it only struck the earth. If it had been a stone, it might have been different. I had no idea there was any one up here except myself."

"It was very kind of you to bow so low to a perfect stranger," said the other, his eyes twinkling humorously. "I suppose it would only be polite for me to follow your example."

"I'll excuse you," said Harry laughing.

"Thank you. That takes a great burden off my mind. I don't like to be outdone in politeness, but really I shouldn't like to tumble over you. My head may be softer than yours. There's one thing clear. We ought to know each other. As you've taken the trouble to come up here, and stumble over me, I really feel as if we ought to strike up a friendship. What do you say?"

"With all my heart," said our hero.

CHAPTER IV.

OSCAR VINCENT.

"Allow me to introduce myself," said the stranger boy. "My name is Oscar Vincent, from Boston, at present a student at the Prescott Academy, at your service."
As he spoke, he doffed his hat and bowed, showing a profusion of chestnut hair, a broad, open brow, and an attractive face, lighted up by a pleasant smile.

Harry felt drawn to him by a feeling which was not long in ripening into friendship.

Imitating the other's frankness, he also took off his hat and replied,—

"Let me introduce myself, in turn, as Harry Walton, junior apprentice in the office of the 'Centreville Gazette,' sometimes profanely called 'printer's devil.'"

"Good!" said Oscar, laughing. "How do you like the business?"

"I think I shall like it, but I have only just started in it. I went into the office for the first time to-day."

"I have an uncle who started as you are doing," said Oscar. "He is now chief editor of a daily paper in Boston."

"Is he?" said Harry, with interest. "Did he find it hard to rise?"

"He is a hard worker. I have heard him say that he used to sit up late of nights during his apprenticeship, studying and improving himself."

"That is what I mean to do," said Harry.

"I don't think he was as lazy as his nephew," said Oscar. "I am afraid if I had been in his place I should have remained in it."

"Are you lazy?" asked Harry, smiling at the other's frankness.

"A little so; that is, I don't improve my opportunities as I might. Father wants to make a lawyer of me so he has put me here, and I am preparing for Harvard."

"I envy you," said Harry. "There is nothing I should like so much as entering college."

"I daresay I shall like it tolerably well," said Oscar; "but I don't hanker after it, as the boy said after swallowing a dose of castor oil. I'll tell you what I should like better—"

"What?" asked Harry, as the other paused.

"I should like to enter the Naval Academy, and qualify myself for the naval service. I always liked the sea."

"Doesn't your father approve of your doing this?"

"He wouldn't mind my entering the navy as an officer, but he is not willing to have me enter the merchant service."

"Then why doesn't he send you to the Naval Academy?"

"Because I can't enter without receiving the appointment from a member of Congress. Our member can only appoint one, and there is no vacancy. So, as I can't go where I want to, I am preparing for Harvard."

"Are you studying Latin and Greek?"

"Yes."

"Have you studied them long?"

"About two years. I was looking over my Greek lesson when you playfully tumbled over me."

"Will you let me look at your book? I never saw a Greek book."

"I sometimes wish I never had," said Oscar; "but that's when I am lazy."

Harry opened the book—a Greek reader—in the middle of an extract from Xenophon, and looked with some awe at the unintelligible letters.

"Can you read it? Can you understand what it means?" he asked, looking up from the book.

"So-so."

"You must know a great deal."

Oscar laughed.

"I wonder what Dr. Burton would say if he heard you," he said.

"Who is he?"

"Principal of our Academy. He gave me a blowing up for my ignorance to-day, because I missed an irregular Greek verb. I'm not exactly a dunce, but I don't think I shall ever be a Greek professor."

"If you speak of yourself that way, what will you think of me? I don't know a word of Latin, of Greek, or any language except my own."

"Because you have had no chance to learn. There's one language I know more about than Latin or Greek."

"English?"

"I mean French; I spent a year at a French boarding-school, three years since."

"What! Have you been in France?"

"Yes; an uncle of mine—in fact, the editor—was going over, and urged father to send me. I learned considerable French, but not much else. I can speak and understand it pretty well."

"How I wish I had had your advantages," said Harry. "How did you like your French schoolmates?"

"They wouldn't come near me at first. Because I was an American they thought I carried a revolver and a dirk-knife, and was dangerous. That is their idea of American boys. When they found I was tame, and carried no deadly weapons, they ventured to speak with me, and after that we got along pretty well."

"How soon do you expect to go to college?"

"A year from next summer. I suppose I shall be ready by that time.
You are going to stay in town, I suppose?"
"Yes, if I keep my place."

"Oh, you'll do that. Then we can see something of each other. You must come up to my room, and see me. Come almost any evening."

"I should like to. Do you live in Dr. Barton's family?"

"No, I hope not."

"Why not?"

"Oh, the Doctor has a way of looking after the fellows that room in the house, and of keeping them at work all the time. That wouldn't suit me. I board at Mrs. Greyson's, at the south-east corner of the church common. Have you got anything to do this evening?"

"Nothing in particular."

"Then come round and take a look at my den, or sanctum I ought to call it; as I am talking to a member of the editorial profession."

"Not quite yet," said Harry, smiling.

"Oh, well that'll come in due time. Will you come?"

"Sha'n't I be disturbing you?"

"Not a bit. My Greek lesson is about finished, and that's all I've got to do this evening. Come round, and we will sit over the fire, and chat like old friends."

"Thank you, Oscar," said Harry, irresistibly attracted by his bright and lively acquaintance, "I shall enjoy calling. I have made no acquaintances yet, and I feel lonely."

"I have got over that," said Oscar. "I am used to being away from home and don't mind it."

The two boys walked together to Oscar's boarding-place. It was a large house, of considerable pretension for a village, and Oscar's room was large and handsomely furnished. But what attracted Harry's attention was not the furniture, but a collection of over a hundred books, ranged on shelves at one end of the room. In his father's house it had always been so difficult to obtain the necessaries of life that books had necessarily been regarded as superfluities, and beyond a dozen volumes which Harry had read and re-read, he was compelled to depend on such as he could borrow. Here again his privileges were scanty, for most of the neighbors were as poorly supplied as his father.

"What a fine library you have, Oscar!" he exclaimed.

"I have a few books," said Oscar. "My father filled a couple of boxes, and sent me. He has a large library."

"This seems a large library to me," said Harry. "My father likes reading, but he is poor, and cannot afford to buy books."

He said that in a matter-of-fact tone, without the least attempt to conceal what many boys would have been tempted to hide. Oscar noted this, and liked his new friend the better for it.

"Yes," he said, "books cost money, and one hasn't always the money to spare."

"Have you read all these books?"

"Not more than half of them. I like reading better than studying, I am afraid. I am reading the Waverley novels now. Have you read any of them?"

"So; I never saw any of them before."

"If you see anything you would like to read, I will lend it to you with pleasure," said Oscar, noticing the interest with which Harry regarded the books.

"Will you?" said Harry, eagerly. "I can't tell you how much obliged
I am. I will take good care of it."
"Oh, I am sure of that. Here, try Ivanhoe. I've just read it, and it's tip-top."

"Thank you; I will take it on your recommendation. What a nice room you have!"

"Yes, it's pretty comfortable. Father told me to fix it up to suit me. He said he wouldn't mind the expense if I would only study."

"I should think anybody might study in such a room as this, and with such a fine collection of books."

"I'm rather lazy sometimes," said Oscar, "but I shall turn over a new leaf some of these days, and astonish everybody. To-night, as I have no studying to do, I'll tell you what we'll do. Did you ever pop corn?"

"Sometimes."

"I've got some corn here, and Ma'am Greyson has a popper. Stay here alone a minute, and I'll run down and get it."

Oscar ran down stairs, and speedily returned with a corn-popper.

"Now we'll have a jolly time," said he. "Draw up that arm-chair, and make yourself at home. If Xenophon, or Virgil, or any of those Greek and Latin chaps call, we'll tell 'em we are transacting important business and can't be disturbed. What do you say?"

"They won't be apt to call on me," said Harry. I haven't the pleasure of knowing them."

"It isn't always a pleasure, I can assure you, Harry. Pass over the corn-popper."

CHAPTER V.

A YOUNG F. F. B.

As the two boys sat in front of the fire, popping and eating the corn, and chatting of one thing and another, their acquaintance improved rapidly. Harry learned that Oscar's father was a Boston merchant, in the Calcutta trade, with a counting-room on Long Wharf. Oscar was a year older than himself, and the oldest child. He had a sister of thirteen, named Florence, and a younger brother, Charlie, now ten. They lived on Beacon Street, opposite the Common. Though Harry had never lived in Boston, be knew that this was a fashionable street, and he had no difficulty in inferring that Mr. Vincent was a rich man. He felt what a wide gulf there was socially between himself and Oscar; one the son of a very poor country farmer, the other the son of a merchant prince. But nothing in Oscar's manner indicated the faintest feeling of superiority, and this pleased Harry. I may as well say, however, that our hero was not one to show any foolish subserviency to a richer boy; he thought mainly of Oscar's superiority in knowledge; and although the latter was far ahead of Harry on this score, he was not one to boast of it.

Harry, in return for Oscar's confidence, acquainted him with his own adventures since he had started out to earn his own living. Oscar was most interested in his apprenticeship to the ventriloquist.

"It must have been jolly fun," he said. "I shouldn't mind travelling round with him myself. Can you perform any tricks?"

"A few," said Harry.

"Show me some, that's a good fellow."

"If you won't show others. Professor Henderson wouldn't like to have his tricks generally known. I could show more if I had the articles he uses. But I can do some without."

"Go ahead, Professor. I'm all attention."

Not having served an apprenticeship to a magician, as Harry did, I will not undertake to describe the few simple tricks which he had picked up, and now exhibited for the entertainment of his companion. It is enough to say that they were quite satisfactory, and that Oscar professed his intention to puzzle his Boston friends with them, when his vacation arrived.

About half-past eight, a knock was heard at the door.

"Come in!" called out Oscar.

The door was opened, and a boy about his own age entered. His name was Fitzgerald Fletcher. He was also a Boston boy, and the son of a retail merchant, doing business on Washington street. His father lived handsomely, and was supposed to be rich. At any rate Fitzgerald supposed him to be so, and was very proud of the fact. He generally let any new acquaintances understand very speedily that his father was a man of property, and that his family moved in the first circles of Boston Society. He cultivated the acquaintance of those boys who belonged to rich families, and did not fail to show the superiority which he felt to those of less abundant means. For example, he liked to be considered intimate with Oscar, as the social position of Mr. Vincent was higher than that of his own family. It gave him an excuse also for calling on Oscar in Boston. He had tried to ingratiate himself also with Oscar's sister Florence, but had only disgusted her with his airs, so that he could not flatter himself with his success in this direction. Oscar had very little liking for him, but as school-fellows they often met, and Fitzgerald often called upon him. On such occasions he treated him politely enough, for it was not in his nature to be rude without cause.

Fitz was elaborately dressed, feeling that handsome clothes would help convey the impression of wealth, which he was anxious to establish. In particular he paid attention to his neckties, of which he boasted a greater variety than any of his school-mates. It was not a lofty ambition, but, such as it was, he was able to gratify it.

"How are you, Fitz?" said Oscar, when he saw who was his visitor.
"Draw up a chair to the fire, and make yourself comfortable."
"Thank you, Oscar," said Fitzgerald, leisurely drawing off a pair of kid gloves; "I thought I would drop in and see you."

"All right! Will you have some popped corn?"

"No, thank you," answered Fitzgerald, shrugging his shoulders. "I don't fancy the article."

"Don't you? Then you don't know what's good."

"Fancy passing round popped corn at a party in Boston," said the other. "How people would stare!"

"Would they? I don't know about that. I think some would be more sensible and eat. But, I beg your pardon, I haven't introduced you to my friend, Harry Walton. Harry, this is a classmate of mine. Fitzgerald Fletcher, Esq., of Boston."

Fitzgerald did not appear to perceive that the title Esq. was sportively added to his name. He took it seriously, and was pleased with it, as a recognition of his social superiority. He bowed ceremoniously to our hero, and said, formally, "I am pleased to make your acquaintance, Mr. Walton."

"Thank you, Mr. Fletcher," replied Harry, bowing in turn.

"I wonder who he is," thought Fitzgerald.

He had no idea of the true position of our young hero, or he would not have wasted so much politeness upon him. The fact was, that Harry was well dressed, having on the suit which had been given him by a friend from the city. It was therefore fashionably cut, and had been so well kept as still to be in very good condition. It occurred to Fitz—to give him the short name he received from his school-fellows—that it might be a Boston friend of Oscar's, just entering the Academy. This might account for his not having met him before. Perhaps he was from an aristocratic Boston family. His intimacy with Oscar rendered it probable, and it might be well to cultivate his acquaintance. On this hint he spoke.

"Are you about to enter the Academy, Mr. Walton?"

"No; I should like to do so, but cannot."

"You are one of Oscar's friends from the city, I suppose, then?"

"Oh no; I am living in Centreville."

"Who can he be?" thought Fitz. With considerable less cordiality in his manner, he continued, impelled by curiosity,—

"I don't think I have met you before."

"No: I have only just come to the village."

Oscar understood thoroughly the bewilderment of his visitor, and enjoyed it. He knew the weakness of Fitz, and he could imagine how his feelings would change when be ascertained the real position of Harry.

"My friend," he explained, "is connected with the 'Centreville
Gazette.'"
"In what capacity?" asked Fitz, in surprise.

"He is profanely termed the 'printer's devil.' Isn't that so, Harry?"

"I believe you are right," said our hero, smiling. He had a suspicion that this relation would shock his new acquaintance.

"Indeed!" ejaculated Fitz, pursing up his lips, and, I was about to say, turning up his nose, but nature had saved him the little trouble of doing that.

"What in the world brings him here, then?" he thought; but there was no need of saying it, for both Oscar and Harry read it in his manner. "Strange that Oscar Vincent, from one of the first families of Boston, should demean himself by keeping company with a low printer boy!"

"Harry and I have had a jolly time popping corn this evening!" said
Oscar, choosing to ignore his school-mate's changed manner.
"Indeed! I can't see what fun there is in it."

"Oh, you've got no taste. Has he, Harry?"

"His taste differs from ours," said our hero, politely.

"I should think so," remarked Fitz, with significant emphasis. "Was that all you had to amuse yourself?"

In using the singular pronoun, he expressly ignored the presence of the young printer.

"No, that wasn't all. My friend Harry has been amusing me with some tricks which he learned while he was travelling round with Professor Henderson, the ventriloquist and magician."

"Really, he is quite accomplished," said Fitz, with a covert sneer. "Pretty company Oscar has taken up with!" he thought. "How long were you in the circus business?" he asked, turning to Harry.

"I never was in the circus business."

"Excuse me. I should say, travelling about with the ventriloquist."

"About three months. I was with him when he performed here last winter."

"Ah! indeed. I didn't go. My father doesn't approve of my attending such common performances. I only attend first-class theatres, and the Italian opera."

"That's foolish," said Oscar. "You miss a good deal of fun, then. I went to Professor Henderson's entertainment, and I now remember seeing you there, Harry. You took money at the door, didn't you?"

"Yes."

"Now I understand what made your face seem so familiar to me, when I saw it this afternoon. By the way, I have never been into a printing office. If I come round to yours, will you show me round?"

"I should be very glad to, Oscar, but perhaps you had better wait till I have been there a little while, and learned the ropes. I know very little about it yet."

"Won't you come too, Fitz?" asked Oscar.

"You must really excuse me," drawled Fitz. "I have heard that a printing office is a very dirty place. I should be afraid of soiling my clothes."

"Especially that stunning cravat."

"Do you like it? I flatter myself it's something a little extra," said Fitz, who was always gratified by a compliment to his cravats.

"Then you won't go?"

"I haven't the slightest curiosity about such a place, I assure you."

"Then I shall have to go alone. Let me know when you are ready to receive me, Harry."

"I won't forget, Oscar."

"I wonder he allows such a low fellow to call him by his first name," thought Fitz. "Really, he has no proper pride."

"Well," he said, rising, "I must be going."

"What's your hurry, Fitz?"

"I've got to write a letter home this evening. Besides, I haven't finished my Greek. Good-evening, Oscar."

"Good-evening, Fitz."

"Good-evening, Mr. Fletcher," said Harry.

"Evening!" ejaculated Fitz, briefly; and without a look at the low "printer-boy," he closed the door and went down stairs.

CHAPTER VI.

OSCAR BECOMES A PROFESSOR

"I am afraid your friend won't thank you for introducing me to him," said Harry, after Fitz had left the room.

"Fitz is a snob," said Oscar. "He makes himself ridiculous by putting on airs, and assuming to be more than he is. His father is in a good business, and may be rich—I don't know about that—but that isn't much to boast of."

"I don't think we shall be very intimate," said Harry, smiling.
"Evidently a printer's apprentice is something very low in his eyes."
"When you are an influential editor he will be willing to recognize you. Let that stimulate your ambition."

"It isn't easy for a half-educated boy to rise to such a position. I feel that I know very little."

"If I can help you any, Harry, I shall be very glad to do it. I'm not much of a scholar, but I can help you a little. For instance, if you wanted to learn French, I could hear your lessons, and correct your exercises."

"Will you?" said Harry, eagerly. "There is nothing I should like better."

"Then I'll tell you what I'll do. You shall buy a French grammar, and come to my room two evenings a week, and recite what you get time to study at home."

"Won't it give you a great deal of trouble, Oscar?"

"Not a bit of it; I shall rather like it. Until you can buy a grammar, I will lend you mine. I'll set you a lesson out of it now."

He took from the book-shelves a French grammar, and inviting Harry to sit down beside him, gave him some necessary explanations as to the pronunciation of words according to the first lesson.

"It seems easy," said Harry. "I can take more than that."

"It is the easiest of the modern languages, to us at least, on account of its having so many words similar to ours."

"What evening shall I come, Oscar?"

"Tuesday and Friday will suit me as well as any. And remember, Harry, I mean to be very strict in discipline. And, by the way, how will it do to call myself Professor?"

"I'll call you Professor if you want me to."

"We'll leave all high titles to Fitz, and I won't use the rod any oftener than it is absolutely necessary."

"All right, Professor Vincent," said Harry laughing, "I'll endeavor to behave with propriety."

"I wonder what they would say at home," said Oscar, "if they knew I had taken up the profession of teacher. Strange as it may seem to you, Harry, I have the reputation in the home-circle of being decidedly lazy. How do you account for it?"

"Great men are seldom appreciated."

"You hit the nail on the head that time—glad I am not the nail, by the way. Henceforth I will submit with resignation to injustice and misconstruction, since I am only meeting with the common fate of great men."

"What time is it, Oscar?"

"Nearly ten."

"Then I will bid you good-night," and Harry rose to go. "I can't tell how much I am obliged to you for your kind offer."

"Just postpone thanks till you find out whether I am a good teacher or not."

"I am sure of that."

"I am not so sure, but I will do what I can for you. Good-night. I'll expect you Friday evening. I shall see Fitz to-morrow. Shall I give him your love?"

"Never mind!" said Harry, smiling. "I'm afraid it wouldn't be appreciated."

"Perhaps not."

As Harry left his lively companion, he felt that he had been most fortunate in securing his friendship—not only that he found him very agreeable and attractive, but he was likely to be of great use to him in promoting his plans of self-education. He had too much good sense not to perceive that the only chance he had of rising to an influential position lay in qualifying himself for it, by enlarging his limited knowledge and improving his mind.

"I have made a good beginning," he thought. "After I have learned something of French, I will take up Latin, and I think Oscar will be willing to help me in that too."

The next morning he commenced work in the printing office. With a few hints from Ferguson, he soon comprehended what he had to do, and made very rapid progress.

"You're getting on fast, Harry," said Ferguson approvingly.

"I like it," said our hero. "I am glad I decided to be a printer."

"I wish I wasn't one," grumbled Clapp, the younger journeyman.

"Don't you like it?"

"Not much. It's hard work and poor pay. I just wish I was in my brother's shoes. He is a bookkeeper in Boston, with a salary of twelve hundred a year, while I am plodding along on fifteen dollars week."

"You may do better some day," said Ferguson.

"Don't see any chance of it."

"If I were in your place, I would save up part of my salary, and by and by have an office, and perhaps a paper of my own."

"Why don't you do it, then?" sneered Clapp.

"Because I have a family to support from my earnings—you have only yourself."

"It doesn't help me any; I can't save anything out of fifteen dollars a week."

"You mean you won't," said Ferguson quietly.

"No I don't. I mean I can't."

"How do you expect I get along, then? I have a wife and two children to support, and only get two dollars a week more than you."

"Perhaps you get into debt."

"No; I owe no man a dollar," said Ferguson emphatically. "That isn't all. I save two dollars a week; so that I actually support four on fifteen dollars a week—your salary. What do you say to that?"

"I don't want to be mean," said Clapp.

"Nor I. I mean to live comfortably, but of course I have to be economical."

"Oh, hang economy!" said Clapp impatiently. "The old man used to lecture me about economy till I got sick of hearing the word."

"It is a good thing, for all that," persisted Ferguson. "You'll think so some day, even if you don't now."

"I guess you mean to run opposition to young Franklin, over there," sneered Clapp, indicating Harry, who had listened to the discussion with not a little interest.

"I think he and I will agree together pretty well," said Ferguson, smiling. "Franklin's a good man to imitate."

"If there are going to be two Franklins in the office, it will be time for me to clear out," returned Clapp.

"You can do better."

"How is that?"

"Become Franklin No. 3."

"You don't catch me imitating any old fogy like that. As far as I know anything about him, he was a mean, stingy old curmudgeon!" exclaimed Clapp with irritation.

"That's rather strong language, Clapp," said Mr. Anderson, looking up from his desk with a smile. "It doesn't correspond with the general estimate of Franklin's character."

"I don't care," said Clapp doggedly, "I wouldn't be like Franklin if
I could. I have too much self-respect."
Ferguson laughed, and Harry wanted to, but feared he should offend the younger journeyman, who evidently had worked himself into a bad humor.

"I don't think you're in any danger," said Ferguson, who did not mind his fellow-workman's little ebullitions of temper.

Clapp scowled, but did not deign to reply, partly, perhaps, because he knew that there was nothing to say.

From the outset Ferguson took a fancy to the young apprentice.

"He's got good, solid ideas," said he to Mr. Anderson, when Harry was absent. "He isn't so thoughtless as most boys of his age. He looks ahead."

"I think you are right in your judgment of him," said Mr. Anderson.
"He promises to be a faithful workman."
"He promises more than that," said Ferguson. "Mark my words, Mr.
Anderson; that boy is going to make his mark some day."
"It is a little too soon to say that, isn't it?"

"No; I judge from what I see. He is industrious and ambitious, and is bound to succeed. The world will hear of him yet."

Mr. Anderson smiled. He liked what he had seen of his new apprentice, but he thought Ferguson altogether too sanguine.

"He's a good, faithful boy," he admitted, "but it takes more than that to rise to distinction. If all the smart boys turned out smart men, they'd be a drug in the market."

But Ferguson held to his own opinion, notwithstanding. Time will show which was right.

The next day Ferguson said, "Harry, come round to my house, and take tea to-night. I've spoken to my wife about you, and she wants to see you."

"Thank you, Mr. Ferguson," said Harry. "I shall be very glad to come."

"I'll wait till you are ready, and you can walk along with me."

"All right; I will be ready in five minutes."

They set out together for Ferguson's modest home, which was about half a mile distant. As they passed up the village street Harry's attention was drawn to two boys who were approaching them. One he recognized at once as Fitzgerald Fletcher. He had an even more stunning necktie than when Harry first met him, and sported a jaunty little cane, which he swung in his neatly gloved hand.

"I wonder if he'll notice me," thought Harry. "At any rate, I won't be wanting in politeness."

"Good-afternoon, Mr. Fletcher," he said, as they met.

Fitzgerald stared at him superciliously, and made the slightest possible nod.

"Who is that?" asked Ferguson.

"It is a boy who has great contempt for printers' devils and low apprentices," answered Harry. "I was introduced to him two evenings ago, but he evidently doesn't care about keeping up the acquaintance."

"Who is that, Fitz?" asked his companion in turn.

"It's a low fellow—a printer's devil," answered Fitz, shortly.

"How do you happen to know him?"

"Oscar Vincent introduced him to me. Oscar's a queer fellow. He belongs to one of the first families in Boston—one of my set, you know, and yet he actually invited that boy to his room."

"He's rather a good-looking boy—the printer."

"Think so?" drawled Fitz. "He's low—all apprentices are. I mean to keep him at a distance."

CHAPTER VII.

A PLEASANT EVENING.

"This is my house," said Ferguson, pausing at the gate.

Harry looked at it with interest.

It was a cottage, containing four rooms, and a kitchen in the ell part. There was a plot of about a quarter of an acre connected with it. Everything about it was neat, though very unpretentious.

"It isn't a palace," said Ferguson, "but," he added cheerfully, "it's a happy home, and from all I've read, that is more than can be said of some palaces. Step right in and make yourself at home."

They entered a tiny entry, and Mrs. Ferguson opened the door of the sitting-room. She was a pleasant-looking woman, and her face wore a smile st welcome.

"Hannah," said Ferguson, "this is our new apprentice, Harry Walton."

"I am glad to see you," she said, offering her hand. "My husband has spoken of you. You are quite welcome, if you can put up with humble fare."

"That is what I have always been accustomed to," said Harry, beginning to feel quite at home.

"Where are the children, Hannah?"

Two children, a boy and a girl, of six and four years respectively, bounded into the room and answered for themselves. They looked shyly at Harry, but before many minutes their shyness had worn off, and the little girl was sitting on his knee, while the boy stood beside him. Harry was fond of children, and readily adapted himself to his young acquaintances.

Supper was soon ready—a plain meal, but one that Harry enjoyed. He could not help comparing Ferguson's plain, but pleasant home, with Clapp's mode of life.

The latter spent on himself as much as sufficed his fellow-workman to support a wife and two children, yet it was easy to see which found the best enjoyment in life.

"How do you like your new business?" asked Mrs. Ferguson, as she handed Harry a cup of tea.

"I like all but the name," said our hero, smiling.

"I wonder how the name came to be applied to a printer's apprentice any more than to any other apprentice," said Mrs. Ferguson.

"I never heard," said her husband. "It seems to me to be a libel upon our trade. But there is one comfort. If you stick to the business, you'll outgrow the name."

"That is lucky; I shouldn't like to be called the wife of a ——. I won't pronounce the word lest the children should catch it."

"What is it, mother?" asked Willie, with his mouth full.

"It isn't necessary for you to know, my boy."

"Do you know Mr. Clapp?" asked Harry.

"I have seen him, but never spoke with him."

"I never asked him round to tea," said Ferguson.

"I don't think he would enjoy it any better than I. His tastes are very different from mine, and his views of life are equally different."

"I should think so," said Harry.

"Now I think you and I would agree very well. Clapp dislikes the business, and only sticks to it because he must get his living in some way. As for me, if I had a sum of money, say five thousand dollars, I would still remain a printer, but in that case I would probably buy out a paper, or start one, and be a publisher, as well as a printer."

"That's just what I should like," said Harry.

"Who knows but we may be able to go into partnership some day, and carry out our plan."

"I would like it," said Harry; "but I am afraid it will be a good while before we can raise the five thousand dollars."

"We don't need as much. Mr. Anderson started on a capital of a thousand dollars, and now he is in comfortable circumstances."

"Then there's hopes for us."

"At any rate I cherish hopes of doing better some day. I shouldn't like always to be a journeyman. I manage to save up a hundred dollars a year. How much have we in the savings bank, Hannah?"

"Between four and five hundred dollars, with interest."

"It has taken me four years to save it up. In five more, if nothing happens, I should be worth a thousand dollars. Journeymen printers don't get rich very fast."

"I hope to have saved up something myself, in five years," said Harry.

"Then our plan may come to pass, after all. You shall be editor, and I publisher."

"I should think you would prefer to be an editor," said his wife.

"I am diffident of my powers in the line of composition," said Ferguson. "I shouldn't be afraid to undertake local items, but when it comes to an elaborate editorial, I should rather leave it in other hands."

"I always liked writing," said Harry. "Of course I have only had a school-boy's practice, but I mean to practise more in my leisure hours."

"Suppose you write a poem for the 'Gazette,' Walton."

Harry smiled.

"I am not ambitious enough for that," he replied. "I will try plain prose."

"Do so," said Ferguson, earnestly. "Our plan may come to something after all, if we wait patiently. It will do no harm to prepare yourself as well as you can. After a while you might write something for the 'Gazette.' I think Mr. Anderson would put it in."

"Shall I sign it P. D.?" asked Harry.

"P. D. stands for Doctor of Philosophy."

"I don't aspire to such a learned title. P. D. also stands for Printer's Devil."

"I see. Well, joking aside, I advise you to improve yourself in writing."

"I will. That is the way Franklin did."

"I remember. He wrote an article, and slipped it under the door of the printing office, not caring to have it known that he was the author."

"Shall I give you a piece of pie, Mr. Walton?" said Mrs. Ferguson.

"Thank you.".

"Me too," said Willie, extending his plate.

"Willie is always fond of pie," said his father, "In a printing office pi is not such a favorite."

When supper was over, Mr. Ferguson showed Harry a small collection of books, about twenty-five in number, neatly arranged on shelves.

"It isn't much of a library," he said, "but a few books are better than none. I should like to buy as many every year; but books are expensive, and the outlay would make too great an inroad upon my small surplus."

"I always thought I should like a library," said Harry, "but my father is very poor, and has fewer books than you. As for me, I have but one book besides the school-books I studied, and that I gained as a school prize—The Life of Franklin."

"If one has few books he is apt to prize them more," said Ferguson, "and is apt to profit by them more."

"Have you read the History of China?" asked Harry, who had been looking over his friend's books.

"No; I have never seen it."

"Why, there it is," said our hero, "In two volumes."

"Take it down," said Ferguson, laughing.

Harry did so, and to his surprise it opened in his hands, and revealed a checker-board.

"You see appearances are deceitful. Can you play checkers?"

"I never tried."

"You will easily learn. Shall I teach you the game?"

"I wish you would."

They sat down; and Harry soon became interested in the game, which requires a certain degree of thought and foresight.

"You will make a good player after a while," said his companion.
"You must come in often and play with me."
"Thank you, I should like to do so. It may not be often, for I am taking lessons in French, and I want to get on as fast as possible."

"I did not know there was any one in the village who gave lessons in French."
"Oh, he's not a professional teacher. Oscar Vincent, one of the Academy boys, is teaching me. I am to take two lessons a week, on Tuesday and Friday evenings."
"Indeed, that is a good arrangement. How did it come about?"

Harry related the particulars of his meeting with Oscar.

"He's a capital fellow," he concluded. "Very different from another boy I met in his room. I pointed him out to you in the street. Oscar seems to be rich, but he doesn't put on any airs, and he treated me very kindly."

"That is to his credit. It's the sham aristocrats that put on most airs. I believe you will make somebody, Walton. You have lost no time in getting to work."

"I have no time to lose. I wish I was in Oscar's place. He is preparing for Harvard, and has nothing to do but to learn."

"I heard a lecturer once who said that the printing office is the poor man's college, and he gave a great many instances of printers who had risen high in the world, particularly in our own country."

"Well, that is encouraging. I should like to have heard the lecture."

"I begin to think, Harry, that I should have done well to follow your example. When I was in your position, I might have studied too, but I didn't realize the importance as I do now. I read some useful books, to be sure, but that isn't like studying."

"It isn't too late now."

Ferguson shook his head.

"Now I have a wife and children," he said. "I am away from them during the day, and the evening I like to pass socially with them."

"Perhaps you would like to be divorced," said his wife, smiling.
"Then you would get time for study."
"I doubt if that would make me as happy, Hannah. I am not ready to part with you just yet. But our young friend here is not quite old enough to be married, and there is nothing to prevent his pursuing his studies. So, Harry, go on, and prepare yourself for your editorial duties."

Harry smiled thoughtfully. For the first time he had formed definite plans for his future. Why should not Ferguson's plans be realized?

"If I live long enough," he said to himself, "I will be an editor, and exert some influence in the world."

At ten o'clock he bade good-night to Mr. and Mrs. Ferguson, feeling that he had passed a pleasant and what might prove a profitable evening.

CHAPTER VIII.

FLETCHER'S VIEWS ON SOCIAL POSITION.

"You are getting on finely, Harry," said Oscar Vincent, a fortnight later. "You do credit to my teaching. As you have been over all the regular verbs now, I will give you a lesson in translating."

"I shall find that interesting," said Harry, with satisfaction.

"Here is a French Reader," said Oscar, taking one down from the shelves. "It has a dictionary at the end. I won't give you a lesson. You may take as much as you have time for, and at the same time three or four of the irregular verbs. You are going about three times as fast as I did when I commenced French."

"Perhaps I have a better teacher than you had," said Harry, smiling.

"I shouldn't wonder," said Oscar. "That explains it to my satisfaction. Well, now the lesson is over, sit down and we'll have a chat. Oh, by the way, there's one thing I want to speak to you about. We've got a debating society at our school. It is called 'The Clionian Society.' Most of the students belong to it. How would you like to join?"

"I should like it very much. Do you think they would admit me?"

"I don't see why not. I'll propose you at the next meeting, Thursday evening. Then the nomination will lie over a week, and be acted upon at the next meeting."

"I wish you would. I never belonged to a debating society, but I should like to learn to speak."

"It's nothing when you're used to it. It's only the first time you know, that troubles you. By Jove! I remember how my knees trembled when I first got up and said Mr. President. I felt as if all eyes were upon me, and I wanted to sink through the floor. Now I can get up and chatter with the best of them. I don't mean that I can make an eloquent speech or anything of that kind, but I can talk at a minute's notice on almost any subject."

"I wish I could."

"Oh, you can, after you've tried a few times. Well, then, it's settled. I'll propose you at the next meeting."

"How lucky I am to have fallen in with you, Oscar."

"I know what you mean. I'm your guide, philosopher, and friend, and all that sort of thing. I hope you'll have proper veneration for me. It's rather a new character for me. Would you believe it, Harry,—at home I am regarded as a rattle-brained chap, instead of the dignified Professor that you know me to be. Isn't it a shame?"

"Great men are seldom appreciated at home, Oscar."

"I know that. I shall have to get a certificate from you, certifying to my being a steady and erudite young man."

"I'll give it with the greatest pleasure."

"Holloa, there's a knock. Come in!" shouted Oscar.

The door opened, and Fitzgerald Fletcher entered the room.

"How are you, Fitz?" said Oscar. "Sit down and make yourself comfortable. You know my friend, Harry Walton, I believe?"

"I believe I had the honor to meet him here one evening," said Fitzgerald stiffly, slightly emphasizing the word "honor."
"I hope you are well, Mr. Fletcher," said Harry, more amused than disturbed by the manner of the aristocratic visitor.

"Thank you, my health is good," said Fitzgerald with equal stiffness, and forthwith turned to Oscar, not deigning to devote any more attention to Harry.

Our hero had intended to remain a short time longer, but, under the circumstances, as Oscar's attention would be occupied by Fletcher, with whom he was not on intimate terms, he thought he might spend the evening more profitably at home in study.

"If you'll excuse me, Oscar," he said, rising, "I will leave you now, as I have something to do this evening."

"If you insist upon it, Harry, I will excuse you. Come round Friday evening."

"Thank you."

"Do you have to work at the printing office in the evening?" Fletcher deigned to inquire.

"No; I have some studying to do."

"Reading and spelling, I suppose," sneered Fletcher.

"I am studying French."

"Indeed!" returned Fletcher, rather surprised. "How can you study it without a teacher?"

"I have a teacher."

"Who is it?"

"Professor Vincent," said Harry, smiling.

"You didn't know that I had developed into a French Professor, did you, Fitz? Well, it's so, and whether it's the superior teaching or not, I can't say, but my scholar is getting on famously."

"It must be a great bore to teach," said Fletcher.

"Not at all. I like it."

"Every one to his taste," said Fitzgerald unpleasantly.

"Good-night, Oscar. Good-night, Mr. Fletcher," said Harry, and made his exit.

"You're a strange fellow, Oscar," said Fletcher, after Harry's departure.

"Very likely, but what particular strangeness do you refer to now?"

"No one but you would think of giving lessons to a printer's devil."

"I don't know about that."

"No one, I mean, that holds your position in society."

"I don't know that I hold any particular position in society."

"Your family live on Beacon Street, and move in the first circles. I am sure my mother would be disgusted if I should demean myself so far as to give lessons to any vulgar apprentice."

"I don't propose to give lessons to any vulgar apprentice."

"You know whom I mean. This Walton is only a printer's devil."

"I don't know that that is any objection to him. It isn't morally wrong to be a printer's devil, is it?"

"What a queer fellow you are, Oscar. Of course I don't mean that. I daresay he's well enough in his place, though he seems to be very forward and presuming, but you know that he's not your equal."

"He is not my equal in knowledge, but I shouldn't be surprised if he would be some time. You'd be astonished to see how fast he gets on."

"I daresay. But I mean in social position."

"It seems to me you can't think of anything but social position."

"Well, it's worth thinking about."

"No doubt, as far as it is deserved. But when it is founded on nothing but money, I wouldn't give much for it."

"Of course we all know that the higher classes are more refined—"

"Than printers' devils and vulgar apprentices, I suppose," put in
Oscar, laughing,
"Yes."

"Well, if refinement consists in wearing kid gloves and stunning neckties, I suppose the higher classes, as you call them, are more refined."

"Do you mean me?" demanded Fletcher, who was noted for the character of his neckties.

"Well, I can't say I don't. I suppose you regard yourself as a representative of the higher classes, don't you?"

"To be sure I do," said Fletcher, complacently.

"So I supposed. Then you see I had a right to refer to you. Now listen to my prediction. Twenty-five years from now, the boy whom you look down upon as a vulgar apprentice will occupy a high position, and you will be glad to number him among your acquaintances."

"Speak for yourself, Oscar," said Fletcher, scornfully.

"I speak for both of us."

"Then I say I hope I can command better associates than this friend of yours."

"You may, but I doubt it."

"You seem to be carried away by him," said Fitzgerald, pettishly. "I don't see anything very wonderful about him, except dirty hands."

"Then you have seen more than I have."

"Of course a fellow who meddles with printer's ink must have dirty hands. Faugh!" said Fletcher, turning up his nose.

At the same time he regarded complacently his own fingers, which he carefully kept aloof from anything that would soil or mar their aristocratic whiteness.

"The fact is, Fitz," said Oscar, argumentatively, "our upper ten, as we call them, spring from just such beginnings as my friend Harry Walton. My own father commenced life in a printing office. But, as you say, he occupies a high position at present."

"Really!" said Fletcher, a little taken aback, for he knew that
Vincent's father ranked higher than his own.
"I daresay your own ancestors were not always patricians."

Fletcher winced. He knew well enough that his father commenced life as a boy in a country grocery, but in the mutations of fortune had risen to be the proprietor of a large dry-goods store on Washington Street. None of the family cared to look back to the beginning of his career. They overlooked the fact that it was creditable to him to have risen from the ranks, though the rise was only in wealth, for Mr. Fletcher was a purse-proud parvenu, who owed all the consideration he enjoyed to his commercial position. Fitz liked to have it understood that he was of patrician lineage, and carefully ignored the little grocery, and certain country relations who occasionally paid a visit to their wealthy relatives, in spite of the rather frigid welcome they received.

"Oh, I suppose there are exceptions," Fletcher admitted reluctantly.
"Your father was smart."
"So is Harry Walton. I know what he is aiming at, and I predict that he will be an influential editor some day."

"Have you got your Greek lesson?" asked Fletcher, abruptly, who did not relish the course the conversation had taken.

"Yes."

"Then I want you to translate a passage for me. I couldn't make it out."

"All right."

Half an hour later Fletcher left Vincent's room.

"What a snob he is!" thought Oscar.

And Oscar was right.

CHAPTER IX.

THE CLIONIAN SOCIETY.

On Thursday evening the main school of the Academy building was lighted up, and groups of boys, varying in age from thirteen to nineteen, were standing in different parts of the room. These were members of the Clionian Society, whose weekly meeting was about to take place.

At eight o'clock precisely the President took his place at the teacher's desk, with the Secretary at his side, and rapped for order. The presiding officer was Alfred DeWitt, a member of the Senior Class, and now nearly ready for college. The Secretary was a member of the same class, by name George Sanborn.

"The Secretary will read the minutes of the last meeting," said the
President, when order had been obtained.
George Sanborn rose and read his report, which was accepted.

"Are any committees prepared to report?" asked the President.

The Finance Committee reported through its chairman, recommending that the fee for admission be established at one dollar, and that each member be assessed twenty-five cents monthly.

"Mr. President," said Fitzgerald Fletcher, rising to his feet, "I would like to say a word in reference to this report."

"Mr. Fletcher has the floor."

"Then, Mr. President, I wish to say that I disagree with the Report of the Committee. I think a dollar is altogether too small. It ought to be at least three dollars, and I myself should prefer five dollars. Again, sir, the Committee has recommended for the monthly assessment the ridiculously small sum of twenty-five cents. I think it ought to be a dollar."

"Mr. President, I should like to ask the gentleman his reason," said Henry Fairbanks, Chairman of the Finance Committee. "Why should we tax the members to such an extent, when the sums reported are sufficient to defray the ordinary expenses of the Society, and to leave a small surplus besides?"

"Mr. President," returned Fletcher, "I will answer the gentleman. We don't want to throw open the Society to every one that can raise a dollar. We want to have an exclusive society."

"Mr. President," said Oscar Vincent, rising, "I should like to ask the gentleman for how many he is speaking. He certainly is not speaking for me. I don't want the Society to be exclusive. There are not many who can afford to pay the exorbitant sums which he desires fixed for admission fee and for monthly assessments, and I for one am not willing to exclude any good fellow who desires to become one of us, but does not boast as heavy a purse as the gentleman who has just spoken."

These remarks of Oscar were greeted with applause, general enough to show that the opinions of nearly all were with him.

"Mr. President," said Henry Fairbanks, "though I am opposed to the gentleman's suggestion, (does he offer it as an amendment?) I have no possible objection to his individually paying the increased rates which he recommends, and I am sure the Treasurer will gladly receive them."

Laughter and applause greeted this hit, and Fletcher once more arose, somewhat vexed at the reception of his suggestion.

"I don't choose—" he commenced.

"The gentleman will address the chair," interrupted the President.

"Mr. President, I don't choose to pay more than the other members, though I can do it without inconvenience. But, as I said, I don't believe in being too democratic. I am not in favor of admitting anybody and everybody into the Society."

"Mr. President," said James Hooper, "I congratulate the gentleman on the flourishing state of his finances. For my own part, I am not ashamed to say that I cannot afford to pay a dollar a month assessment, and, were it required, I should be obliged to offer my resignation."

"So much the better," thought Fitzgerald, for, as Hooper was poor, and went coarsely clothed, he looked down upon him. Fortunately for himself he did not give utterance to his thought.

"Does Mr. Fletcher put his recommendation into the form of an amendment?" asked, the President.

"I do."

"Be kind enough to state it, then."

Fletcher did so, but as no one seconded it, no action was of course taken.

"Nominations for membership are now in order," said the President.

"I should like to propose my friend Henry Walton."

"Who is Henry Walton?" asked a member.

"Mr. President, may I answer the gentleman?" asked Fitzgerald Fletcher, rising to his feet.
"As the nominee is not to be voted upon this evening, it is not in order."

"Mr. President," said Oscar, "I should be glad to have the gentleman report his information."

"Mr. Fletcher may speak if he desires it, but as the name will be referred to the Committee on Nominations, it is hardly necessary."

"Mr. President, I merely wish to inform the Society, that Mr. Walton occupies the dignified position of printer's devil in the office of the 'Centreville Gazette.'"

"Mr. President," said Oscar, "may I ask the indulgence of the Society long enough to say that I am quite aware of the fact. I will add that Mr. Walton is a young man of excellent abilities, and I am confident will prove an accession to the Society."

"I cannot permit further remarks on a matter which will come in due course before the Committee on Nominations," said the President.

"The next business in order is the debate."

Of the debate, and the further proceedings, I shall not speak, as they are of no special interest. But after the meeting was over, groups of members discussed matters which had come up during the evening. Fletcher approached Oscar Vincent, and said, "I can't see, Oscar, why you are trying to get that printer's devil into our Society."

"Because he's a good fellow, and smart enough to do us credit."

"If there were any bootblacks in Centreville I suppose you'd be proposing them?" said Fletcher with a sneer.

"I might, if they were as smart as my friend Walton."

"You are not very particular about your friends," said Fletcher in the same tone.

"I don't ask them to open their pocket-books, and show me how much money they have."

"I prefer to associate with gentlemen."

"So do I."

"Yet you associate with that printer's devil."

"I consider him a gentleman."

Fletcher laughed scornfully.

"You have strange ideas of a gentleman," he said.

"I hold the same," said James Hooper, who had come up in time to hear the last portion of the conversation. "I don't think a full purse is the only or the chief qualification of a gentleman. If labor is to be a disqualification, then I must resign all claims to be considered a gentleman, as I worked on a farm for two years before coming to school, and in that way earned the money to pay my expenses here."

Fletcher turned up his nose, but did not reply.

Hooper was a good scholar and influential in the Society, but in Fletcher's eyes he was unworthy of consideration.

"Look here, Fletcher,—what makes you so confoundedly exclusive is your ideas?" asked Henry Fairbanks.

"Because I respect myself," said Fletcher in rather a surly tone.

"Then you have one admirer," said Fairbanks.

"What do you mean by that?" asked Fletcher, suspiciously.

"Nothing out of the way. I believe in self-respect, but I don't see how it is going to be endangered by the admission of Oscar's friend to the Society."

"Am I expected to associate on equal terms with a printer's devil?"

"I can't answer for you. As for me, if he is a good fellow, I shall welcome him to our ranks. Some of our most eminent men have been apprenticed to the trade of printer. I believe, after all, it is the name that has prejudiced you."

"No it isn't. I have seen him."

"Henry Walton?"

"Yes."

"Where?"

"In Oscar's room."

"Well?"

"I don't like his appearance."

"What's the matter with his appearance?" asked Oscar.

"He looks low."

"That's where I must decidedly contradict you, Fitz, and I shall appeal confidently to the members of the Society when they come to know him, as they soon will, for I am sure no one else shares your ridiculous prejudices. Harry Walton, in my opinion, is a true gentleman, without reference to his purse, and he is bound to rise hereafter, take my word for it."

"There's plenty of room for him to rise," said Fletcher with a sneer.

"That is true not only of him, but of all of us, I take it."

"Do you refer to me?"

"Oh no," said Oscar with sarcasm. "I am quite aware that you are at the pinnacle of eminence, even if you do flunk in Greek occasionally."

Fitzgerald had failed in the Greek recitation during the day, and that in school parlance is sometimes termed a "flunk." He bit his lip in mortification at this reference, and walked away, leaving Oscar master of the situation.

"You had the best of him there, Vincent," said George Sanborn. "He has gone off in disgust."

"I like to see Fletcher taken down," said Henry Fairbanks. "I never saw a fellow put on so many airs. He is altogether too aristocratic to associate with ordinary people."

"Yes," said Oscar, "he has a foolish pride, which I hope he will some time get rid of."

"He ought to have been born in England, and not in a republic."

"If he had been born in England, he would have been unhappy unless he had belonged to the nobility," said Alfred DeWitt.

"Look here, boys," said Tom Carver, "what do you say to mortifying Fitz's pride?"

"Have you got a plan in view, Tom? If so, out with it."

"Yes: you know the pedler that comes into town about once a month to buy up rags, and sell his tinwares."

"I have seen him. Well, what of him?"

"He is coming early next week. Some of us will see him privately, and post him up as to Fitz's relations and position, and hire him to come up to school, and inquire for Fitz, representing himself as his cousin. Of course Fitz will deny it indignantly, but he will persist and show that he knows all about the family."

"Good! Splendid!" exclaimed the boys laughing. "Won't Fitz be raving?"

"There's no doubt about that. Well, boys, I'll arrange it all, if you'll authorize me."

"Go ahead, Tom. You can draw upon us for the necessary funds."

Fletcher had retired to his room, angry at the opposition his proposal had received, and without any warning of the humiliation which awaited him.

CHAPTER X.

THE TIN-PEDLER.

Those of my readers who live in large cities are probably not familiar with the travelling tin-pedler, who makes his appearance at frequent intervals in the country towns and villages of New England. His stock of tinware embraces a large variety of articles for culinary purposes, ranging from milk-pans to nutmeg-graters. These are contained in a wagon of large capacity, in shape like a box, on which he sits enthroned a merchant prince. Unlike most traders, he receives little money, most of his transactions being in the form of a barter, whereby be exchanges his merchandise for rags, white and colored, which have accumulated in the household, and are gladly traded off for bright tinware. Behind the cart usually depend two immense bags, one for white, the other for colored rags, which, in time, are sold to paper manufacturers. It may be that the very paper on which this description is printed, was manufactured from rags so collected.

Abner Bickford was the proprietor of such an establishment as I have described. No one, at first sight, would have hesitated to class him as a Yankee. He was long in the limbs, and long in the face, with a shrewd twinkle in the eye, a long nose, and the expression of a man who respected himself and feared nobody. He was unpolished, in his manners, and knew little of books, but he belonged to the same resolute and hardy type of men who in years past sprang to arms, and fought bravely for an idea. He was strong in his manhood, and would have stood unabashed before a king. Such was the man who was to mortify the pride of Fitzgerald Fletcher.

Tom Carver watched for his arrival in Centreville, and walking up to his cart, accosted him.

"Good-morning, Mr. Bickford."

"Good-mornin', young man. You've got the advantage of me. I never saw you before as I know of."

"I am Tom Carver, at your service."

"Glad to know you. Where do you live? Maybe your wife would like some tinware this mornin'?" said Abner, relaxing his gaunt features into a smile.

"She didn't say anything about it when I came out," said Tom, entering into the joke.

"Maybe you'd like a tin-dipper for your youngest boy?"

"Maybe I would, if you've got any to give away."

"I see you've cut your eye-teeth. Is there anything else I can do for you? I'm in for a trade."

"I don't know, unless I sell myself for rags."

"Anything for a trade. I'll give you two cents a pound."

"That's too cheap. I came to ask your help in a trick we boys want to play on one of our number."

"Sho! you don't say so. That aint exactly in my line."

"I'll tell you all about it. There's a chap at our school—the Academy, you know—who's awfully stuck up. He's all the time bragging about belonging to a first family in Boston, and turning up his nose at poorer boys. We want to mortify him."

"Just so!" said Abner, nodding. "Drive ahead!"

"Well, we thought if you'd call at the school and ask after him, and pretend he was a cousin of yours, and all that, it would make him mad."

"Oh, I see," said Abner, nodding, "he wouldn't like to own a tin-pedler for his cousin."

"No," said Tom; "he wants us to think all his relations are rich. I wouldn't mind at all myself," he added, it suddenly occurring to him that Abner's feelings might be hurt.

"Good!" said Abner, "I see you aint one of the stuck-up kind. I've got some relations in Boston myself, that are rich and stuck up. I never go near 'em. What's the name of this chap you're talkin' about?"

"Fletcher—Fitzgerald Fletcher."

"Fletcher!" repeated Abner. "Whew! well, that's a joke!"

"What's a joke?" asked Tom, rather surprised.

"Why, he is my relation—a sort of second cousin. Why, my mother and his father are own cousins. So, don't you see we're second cousins?"

"That's splendid!" exclaimed Tom. "I can hardly believe it."

"It's so. My mother's name was Fletcher—Roxanna Fletcher—afore she married. Jim Fletcher—this boy's father—used to work in my grandfather's store, up to Hampton, but he got kinder discontented, and went off to Boston, where he's been lucky, and they do say he's mighty rich now. I never go nigh him, 'cause I know he looks down on his country cousins, and I don't believe in pokin' my nose in where I aint wanted."

"Then you are really and truly Fitz's cousin?"

"If that's the boy's name. Seems to me it's a kinder queer one. I s'pose it's a fust-claas name. Sounds rather stuck up."

"Won't the boys roar when they hear about it! Are you willing to enter into our plan?"

"Well," said Abner, "I'll do it. I can't abide folks that's stuck up. I'd rather own a cousin like you."

"Thank you, Mr. Bickford."

"When do you want me to come round?"

"How long do you stay in town?"

"Well, I expect to stop overnight at the tavern; I can't get through in one day."

"Then come round to the Academy to-morrow morning, about half-past eight. School don't begin till nine, but the boys will be playing ball alongside. Then we'll give you an introduction to your cousin."

"That'll suit me well enough. I'll come."

Tom Carver returned in triumph, and communicated to the other boys the arrangement be had made with Mr. Bickford, and his unexpected discovery of the genuine relationship that existed between Fitz and the tin-pedler. His communication was listened to with great delight, and no little hilarity, and the boys discussed the probable effect of the projected meeting.

"Fitz will be perfectly raving," said Henry Fairbanks. "There's nothing that will take down his pride so much."

"He'll deny the relationship, probably," said Oscar.

"How can he?"

"He'll do it. See if he don't. It would be death to all his aristocratic claims to admit it."

"Suppose it were yourself, Oscar?"

"I'd say, 'How are you, cousin? How's the the business?'" answered
Oscar, promptly.
"I believe you would, Oscar. There's nothing of the snob about you."

"I hope not."

"Yet your family stands as high as Fletcher's."

"That's a point I leave to others to discuss," said Oscar. "My father is universally respected, I am sure, but he rose from the ranks. He was once a printer's devil, like my friend Harry Walton. Wouldn't it be ridiculous in me to turn up my nose at Walton, just because be stands now where my father did thirty years ago? It would be the same thing as sneering at father."

"Give us your hand, Oscar," said Henry Fairbanks. "You've got no nonsense about you—I like you."

"I'm not sure whether your compliment is deserved, Henry," said
Oscar, "but if I have any nonsense it isn't of that kind."
"Do you believe Fitz has any suspicion that he has a cousin in the tin business?"

"No; I don't believe he has. He must know he has poor relations, living in the country, but he probably thinks as little as possible about them. As long as they don't intrude themselves upon his greatness, I suppose he is satisfied."

"And as long as no one suspects that he has any connection with such plebeians."

"Of course."

"What sort of a man is this tin-pedler, Tom?" asked Oscar.

"He's a pretty sharp fellow—not educated, or polished, you know, but he seems to have some sensible ideas. He said he had never seen the Fletchers; because he didn't want to poke his nose in where he wasn't wanted. He showed his good sense also by saying that he had rather have me for a cousin than Fitz."

"That isn't a very high compliment—I'd say the same myself."

"Thank you, Oscar. Your compliment exalts me. You won't mind my strutting a little."

And Tom humorously threw back his head, and strutted about with mock pride.

"To be sure," said Oscar, "you don't belong to one of the first families of Boston, like our friend, Fitz."

"No, I belong to one of the second families. You can't blame me, for I can't help it."

"No, I won't blame you, but of course I consider you low."

"I am afraid, Tom, I haven't got any cousins in the tin trade, like Fitz."

"Poor Fitz! he little dreams of his impending trial. If he did, I am afraid he wouldn't sleep a wink to-night."

"I wish I thought as much of myself as Fitz does," said Henry Fairbanks. "You can see by his dignified pace, and the way he tosses his head, how well satisfied he is with being Fitzgerald Fletcher, Esq."

"I'll bet five cents he won't strut round so much to-morrow afternoon," said Tom, "after his interview with his new cousin. But hush, boys! Not a word more of this. There's Fitz coming up the hill. I wouldn't have him suspect what's going on, or he might defeat our plans by staying away."

CHAPTER XI.

FITZ AND HIS COUSIN.

The next morning at eight the boys began to gather in the field beside the Seminary. They began to play ball, but took little interest in the game, compared with the "tragedy in real life," as Tom jocosely called it, which was expected soon to come off.

Fitz appeared upon the scene early. In fact one of the boys called for him, and induced him to come round to school earlier than usual. Significant glances were exchanged when he made his appearance, but Fitz suspected nothing, and was quite unaware that he was attracting more attention than usual.

Punctually at half-past eight, Abner Bickford with his tin-cart appeared in the street, and with a twitch of the rein began to ascend the Academy Hill.

"Look there," said Tom Carver, "the tin-pedler's coming up the hill. Wonder if he expects to sell any of his wares to us boys. Do you know him, Fitz?"

"I!" answered Fitzgerald with a scornful look, "what should I know of a tin-pedler?"

Tom's mouth twitched, and his eyes danced with the anticipation of fun.

By this time Mr. Bickford had brought his horse to a halt, and jumping from his box, approached the group of boys, who suspended their game.

"We don't want any tinware," said one of the boys, who was not in the secret.

"Want to know! Perhaps you haven't got tin enough to pay for it.
Never mind, I'll buy you for old rags, at two cents a pound."
"He has you there, Harvey," said Tom Carver. "Can I do anything for you, sir?"

"Is your name Fletcher?" asked Abner, not appearing to recognize Tom.

"Why, he wants you, Fitz!" said Harvey, in surprise.

"This gentleman's name is Fletcher," said Tom, placing his hand on the shoulder of the astonished Fitzgerald.

"Not Fitz Fletcher?" said Abner, interrogatively.

"My name is Fitzgerald Fletcher," said the young Bostonian, haughtily, "but I am at a loss to understand why you should desire to see me."

Abner advanced with hand extended, his face lighted up with an expansive grin.

"Why, Cousin Fitz," he said heartily, "do you mean to say you don't know me?"

"Sir," said Fitzgerald, drawing back, "you are entirely mistaken in the person. I don't know you."

"I guess it's you that are mistaken, Fitz," said the pedler, familiarly; "why, don't you remember Cousin Abner, that used to trot you on his knee when you was a baby? Give us your hand, in memory of old times."

"You must be crazy," said Fitzgerald, his cheeks red with indignation, and all the more exasperated because he saw significant smiles on the faces of his school-companions.

"I s'pose you was too young to remember me," said Abner. "I haint seen you for ten years."

"Sir," said Fitz, wrathfully, "you are trying to impose upon me. I am a native of Boston."

"Of course you be," said the imperturbable pedler. "Cousin Jim—that's your father—went to Boston when he was a boy, and they do say he's worked his way up to be a mighty rich man. Your father is rich, aint he?"

"My father is wealthy, and always was," said Fitzgerald.

"No he wasn't, Cousin Fitz," said Abner. "When he was a boy, he used to work in grandfather's store up to Hampton; but he got sort of discontented and went to Boston. Did you ever hear him tell of his cousin Roxanna? That's my mother."

"I see that you mean to insult me, fellow," said Fitz, pale with passion. "I don't know what your object is, in pretending that I am your relation. If you want any pecuniary help—"

"Hear the boy talk!" said the pedler, bursting into a horse laugh. "Abner Bickford don't want no pecuniary help, as you call it. My tin-cart'll keep me, I guess."

"You needn't claim relationship with me," said Fitzgerald, scornfully; "I haven't any low relations."

"That's so," said Abner, emphatically; "but I aint sure whether I can say that for myself."

"Do you mean to insult me?"

"How can I? I was talkin' of my relations. You say you aint one of 'em."

"I am not."

"Then you needn't go for to put on the coat. But you're out of your reckoning, I guess. I remember your mother very well. She was Susan Baker."

"Is that true, Fitz?"

"Ye—es," answered Fitz, reluctantly.

"I told you so," said the pedler, triumphantly.

"Perhaps he is your cousin, after all," said Henry Fairbanks.

"I tell you he isn't," said Fletcher, impetuously.

"How should he know your mother's name, then, Fitz?" asked Tom.

"Some of you fellows told him," said Fitzgerald.

"I can say, for one, that I never knew it," said Tom.

"Nor I."

"Nor I."

"We used to call her Sukey Baker," said Abner. "She used to go to the deestrict school along of Mother. They was in the same class. I haven't seen your mother since you was a baby. How many children has she got?"

"I must decline answering your impertinent questions." said Fitzgerald, desperately. He began to entertain, for the first time, the horrible suspicion that the pedler's story might be true—that he might after all be his cousin. But he resolved that he never would admit it—NEVER! Where would be his pretentious claims to aristocracy—where his pride—if this humiliating discovery were made? Judging of his school-fellows and himself, he feared that they would look down upon him.

"You seem kind o' riled to find that I am your cousin," said Abner. "Now, Fitz, that's foolish. I aint rich, to be sure, but I'm respectable. I don't drink nor chew, and I've got five hundred dollars laid away in the bank."

"You're welcome to your five hundred dollars," said Fitz, in what was meant to be a tone of withering sarcasm.

"Am I? Well, I'd orter be, considerin' I earned it by hard work. Seems to me you've got high notions, Fitz. Your mother was kind of flighty, and I've heard mine say Cousin Jim—that's your father—was mighty sot up by gettin' rich. But seems to me you ought not to deny your own flesh and blood."

"I don't know who you refer to, sir."

"Why, you don't seem to want to own me as your cousin."

"Of course not. You're only a common tin-pedler."

"Well, I know I'm a tin-pedler, but that don't change my bein' your cousin."

"I wish my father was here to expose your falsehood."

"Hold on there!" said Abner. "You're goin' a leetle too far. I don't let no man, nor boy neither, charge me with lyin', if he is my cousin, I don't stand that, nohow."

There was something in Abner's tone which convinced Fitzgerald that he was in earnest, and that he himself must take care not to go too far.

"I don't wish to have anything more to say to you," said Fitz."

"I say, boys," said Abner, turning to the crowd who had now formed a circle around the cousins, "I leave it to you if it aint mean for Fitz to treat me in that way. If he was to come to my house, that aint the way I'd treat him."

"Come, Fitz," said Tom, "you are not behaving right. I would not treat my cousin that way."

"He isn't my cousin, and you know it," said Fitz, stamping with rage.

"I wish I wasn't," said Abner. "If I could have my pick, I'd rather have him," indicating Tom. "But blood can't be wiped out. We're cousins, even if we don't like it."

"Are you quite sure you are right about this relationship?" asked Henry Fairbanks, gravely. "Fitz, here, says he belongs to one of the first families of Boston."

"Well, I belong to one of the first families of Hampton," said Abner, with a grin. "Nobody don't look down on me, I guess."

"You hear that, Fitz," said Oscar. "Be sensible, and shake hands with your cousin."

"Yes, shake hands with your cousin!" echoed the boys.

"You all seem to want to insult me," said Fitz, sullenly.

"Not I," said Oscar, "and I'll prove it—will you shake hands with me, sir?"

"That I will," said Abner, heartily. "I can see that you're a young gentleman, and I wish I could say as much for my cousin, Fitz."

Oscar's example was followed by the rest of the boys, who advanced in turn, and shook hands with the tin-pedler.

"Now Fitz, it's your turn," said Tom.

"I decline," said Fitz, holding his hands behind his back.

"How much he looks like his marm did when she was young," said Abner.
"Well, boys, I can't stop no longer. I didn't think Cousin Fitz
would be so stuck up, just because his father's made some money.
Good-mornin'!"
"Three cheers for Fitz's cousin!" shouted Tom.

They were given with a will, and Mr. Bickford made acknowledgment by a nod and a grin.

"Remember me to your mother when you write, Cousin Fitz," he said at parting.

Fitz was too angry to reply. He walked off sullenly, deeply mortified and humiliated, and for weeks afterward nothing would more surely throw him into a rage than any allusion to his cousin the tin-pedler. One good effect, however, followed. He did not venture to allude to the social position of his family in presence of his school-mates, and found it politic to lay aside some of his airs of superiority.

CHAPTER XII.

HARRY JOINS THE CLIONIAN SOCIETY.

A week later Harry Walton received the following note:—

"Centreville, May 16th, 18—,
"Dear Sir: At the last meeting of the Clionian

Society you were elected a member. The next meeting will be held on Thursday evening, in the Academy building.

"Yours truly,

"GEORGE SANBORN,

"Secretary.

"MR. HARRY WALTON."

Our hero read this letter with satisfaction. It would be pleasant for him to become acquainted with the Academy students, but he thought most of the advantages which his membership would afford him in the way of writing and speaking. He had never attempted to debate, and dreaded attempting it for the first time; but he knew that nothing desirable would be accomplished without effort, and he was willing to make that effort.

"What have you there, Walton?" asked Clapp, noticing the letter which he held in his hand.

"You can read it if you like," said Harry.

"Humph!" said Clapp; "so you are getting in with the Academy boys?"

"Why shouldn't he?" said Ferguson.

"Oh, they're a stuck-up set."

"I don't find them so—that is, with one exception," said Harry.

"They are mostly the sones of rich men, and look down on those who have to work for a living."

Clapp was of a jealous and envious disposition, and he was always fancying slights where they were not intended.

"If I thought so," said Harry, "I would not join the Society, but as they have elected me, I shall become a member, and see how things turn out."

"It is a good plan, Harry," said Ferguson. "It will be a great advantage to you."

"I wish I had a chance to attend the Academy for a couple of years," said our hero, thoughtfully.

"I don't," said Clapp. "What's the good of studying Latin and Greek, and all that rigmarole? It won't bring you money, will it?"

"Yes," said Ferguson. "Education will make a man more competent to earn money, at any rate in many cases. I have a cousin, who used to go to school with me, but his father was able to send him to college. He is now a lawyer in Boston, making four or five times my income. But it isn't for the money alone that an education is worth having. There is a pleasure in being educated."

"So I think," said Harry.

"I don't see it," said Clapp. "I wouldn't be a bookworm for anybody. There's Walton learning French. What good is it ever going to do him?"

"I can tell you better by and by, when I know a little more," said
Harry. "I am only a beginner now."
"Dr. Franklin would never have become distinguished if he had been satisfied with what he knew as an apprentice," said Ferguson.

"Oh, if you're going to bring up Franklin again, I've got through," said Clapp with a sneer. "I forgot that Walton was trying to be a second Franklin."

"I don't see much chance of it," said Harry, good-humoredly. "I should like to be if I could."

Clapp seemed to be in an ill-humor, and the conversation was not continued. He had been up late the night before with Luke Harrison, and both had drank more than was good for them. In consequence, Clapp had a severe headache, and this did not improve his temper.

"Come round Thursday evening, Harry," said Oscar Vincent, "and go to the Society with me. I will introduce you to the fellows. It will be less awkward, you know."

"Thank you, Oscar. I shall be glad to accept your escort."

When Thursday evening came, Oscar and Harry entered the Society hall arm in arm. Oscar led his companion up to the Secretary and introduced him.

"I am glad to see you, Mr. Walton," said he. "Will you sign your name to the Constitution? That is all the formality we require."

"Except a slight pecuniary disbursement," added Oscar.

"How much is the entrance fee?" asked Harry.

"One dollar. You win pay that to the Treasurer."

Oscar next introduced our hero to the President, and some of the leading members, all of whom welcomed him cordially.

"Good-evening, Mr. Fletcher," said Harry, observing that young gentleman near him.

"Good-evening, sir," said Fletcher stiffly, and turned on his heel without offering his hand.

"Fletcher don't feel well," whispered Oscar. "He had a visit from a poor relation the other day—a tin-pedler—and it gave such a shock to his sensitive system that he hasn't recovered from it yet."

"I didn't imagine Mr. Fletcher had such a plebeian relative," said
Harry.
"Nor did any of us. The interview was rich. It amused us all, but what was sport to us was death to poor Fitz. You have only to make the most distant allusion to a tin-pedler in his hearing, and he will become furious."

"Then I will be careful."

"Oh, it won't do any harm. The fact was, the boy was getting too overbearing, and putting on altogether too many airs. The lesson will do him good, or ought to."

Here the Society was called to order, and Oscar and Harry took their seats.

The exercises proceeded in regular order until the President announced a declamation by Fitzgerald Fletcher.

"Mr. President," said Fletcher, rising, "I must ask to be excused. I have not had time to prepare a declamation."

"Mr. President," said Tom Carver, "under the circumstances I hope you will excuse Mr. Fletcher, as during the last week he has had an addition to his family."

There was a chorus of laughter, loud and long, at this sally. All were amused except Fletcher himself, who looked flushed and provoked.

"Mr. Fletcher is excused," said the President, unable to refrain from smiling. "Will any member volunteer to speak in his place? It will be a pity to have our exercises incomplete."

Fletcher was angry, and wanted to be revenged on somebody. A bright idea came to him. He would place the "printer's devil," whose admission to the Society he resented, in an awkward position. He rose with a malicious smile upon his face.

"Mr. President," he said, "doubtless Mr. Walton, the new member who has done us the honor to join our society, will be willing to supply my place."

"We shall certainly be glad to hear a declamation from Mr. Walton, though it is hardly fair to call upon him at such short notice."

"Can't you speak something, Harry?" whispered Oscar. "Don't do it, unless you are sure you can get through."

Harry started in surprise when his name was first mentioned, but he quickly resolved to accept his duty. He had a high reputation at home for speaking, and he had recently learned a spirited poem, familiar, no doubt, to many of my young readers, called "Shamus O'Brien." It is the story of an Irish volunteer, who was arrested for participating in the Irish rebellion of '98, and is by turns spirited and pathetic. Harry had rehearsed it to himself only the night before, and he had confidence in a strong and retentive memory. At the President's invitation he rose to his feet, and said, "Mr. President, I will do as well as I can, but I hope the members of the Society will make allowance for me, as I have had no time for special preparation."

All eyes were fixed with interest upon our hero, as he advanced to the platform, and, bowing composedly, commenced his declamation. It was not long before that interest increased, as Harry proceeded in his recitation. He lost all diffidence, forgot the audience, and entered thoroughly into the spirit of the piece. Especially when, in the trial scene, Shamus is called upon to plead guilty or not guilty, Harry surpassed himself, and spoke with a spirit and fire which brought down the house. This is the passage:—

"My lord, if you ask me, if in my life-time
I thought any treason, or did any crime,

That should call to my cheek, as I stand alone here,
The hot blush of shame, or the coldness of fear,
Though I stood by the grave to receive my death-blow,
Before God and the world I would answer you, no!
But if you would ask me, as I think it like,
If in the rebellion I carried a pike,
An' fought for ould Ireland from the first to the close,
An' shed the heart's blood of her bitterest foes,
I answer you, yes; and I tell you again,
Though I stand here to perish, it's my glory that then
In her cause I was willing my veins should run dhry,
An' that now for her sake I am ready to die."

After the applause had subsided, Harry proceeded, and at the conclusion of the declamation, when he bowed modestly and left the platform, the hall fairly shook with the stamping, in which all joined except Fletcher, who sat scowling with dissatisfaction at a result so different from his hopes. He had expected to bring discomfiture to our hero. Instead, he had given him an opportunity to achieve a memorable triumph.

"You did yourself credit, old boy!" said Oscar, seizing and wringing the hand of Harry, as the latter resumed his seat. "Why, you ought to go on the stage!"

"Thank you," said Harry; "I am glad I got through well."

"Isn't Fitz mad, though? He thought you'd break down. Look at him!"

Harry looked over to Fletcher, who, with a sour expression, was sitting upright, and looking straight before him.

"He don't look happy, does he?" whispered Oscar, comically.

Harry came near laughing aloud, but luckily for Fletcher's peace of mind, succeeded in restraining himself.

"He won't call you up again in a hurry; see if he does," continued Oscar.

"I am sure we have all been gratified by Mr. Walton's spirited declamation," said the President, rising. "We congratulate ourselves upon adding so fine a speaker to our society, and hope often to have the pleasure of hearing him declaim."

There was a fresh outbreak of applause, after which the other exercises followed. When the meeting was over the members of the Society crowded around Harry, and congratulated him on his success. These congratulations he received so modestly, as to confirm the favorable impression he had made by his declamation.

"By Jove! old fellow," said Oscar, as they were walking home, "I am beginning to be proud of you. You are doing great credit to your teacher."

"Thank you, Professor," said Harry. "Don't compliment me too much, or I may become vain, and put on airs."

"If you do, I'll get Fitz to call, and remind you that you are only a printer's devil, after all."

CHAPTER XIII.

VACATION BEGINS AT THE ACADEMY.

Not long after his election as a member of the Clionian Society, the summer term of the Prescott Academy closed. The examination took place about the tenth of June, and a vacation followed, lasting till the first day of September. Of course, the Clionian Society, which was composed of Academy students, suspended its meetings for the same length of time. Indeed, the last meeting for the season took place during the first week in June, as the evenings were too short and too warm, and the weather was not favorable to oratory. At the last meeting, an election was held of officers to serve for the following term. The same President and Vice-President were chosen; but as the Secretary declined to serve another term, Harry Walton, considerably to his surprise, found himself elected in his place.

Fitzgerald Fletcher did not vote for him. Indeed, he expressed it as his opinion that it was a shame to elect a "printer's devil" Secretary of the Society.

"Why is it?" said Oscar. "Printing is a department of literature, and the Clionian is a literary society, isn't it?"

"Of course it is a literary society, but a printer's devil is not literary."

"He's as literary as a tin-pedler," said Tom Carver, maliciously.

Fletcher turned red, but managed to say, "And what does that prove?"

"We don't object to you because you are connected with the tin business."

"Do you mean to insult me?" demanded Fletcher, angrily. "What have I to do with the tin business?"

"Oh, I beg pardon, it's your cousin that's in it."

"I deny the relationship," said Fletcher, "and I will thank you not to refer again to that vulgar pedler."

"Really, Fitz, you speak rather roughly, considering he's your cousin. But as to Harry Walton, he's a fine fellow, and he has an excellent handwriting, and I was very glad to vote for him."

Fitzgerald walked away, not a little disgusted, as well at the allusion to the tin-pedler, as at the success of Harry Walton in obtaining an office to which he had himself secretly aspired. He had fancied that it would sound well to put "Secretary of the Clionian Society" after his name, and would give him increased consequence at home. As to the tin-pedler, it would have relieved his mind to hear that Mr. Bickford had been carried off suddenly by an apoplectic fit, and notwithstanding the tie of kindred, he would not have taken the trouble to put on mourning in his honor.

Harry Walton sat in Oscar Vincent's room, on the last evening of the term. He had just finished reciting the last French lesson in which he would have Oscar's assistance for some time to come.

"You have made excellent progress," said Oscar. "It is only two months since you began French, and now you take a long lesson in translation."

"That is because I have so good a teacher. But do you think I can get along without help during the summer?"

"No doubt of it. You may find some difficulties, but those you can mark, and I will explain when I come back. Or I'll tell you what is still better. Write to me, and I'll answer. Shall I write in French?"

"I wish you would, Oscar."

"Then I will. I'm rather lazy with the pen, but I can find time for you. Besides, it will be a good way for me to keep up my French."

"Shall you be in Boston all summer, Oscar?"

"No; our family has a summer residence at Nahant, a sea-shore place twelve miles from Boston. Then I hope father will let me travel about a little on my own account. I want to go to Saratoga and Lake George."

"That would be splendid."

"I wish you could go with me, Harry."

"Thank you, Oscar, but perhaps you can secure Fletcher's company. That will be much better than that of a 'printer's devil' like myself."

"It may show bad taste, but I should prefer your company, notwithstanding your low employment."

"Thank you, Oscar. I am much obliged."

"Fitz has been hinting to me how nice it would be for us to go off somewhere together, but I don't see it in that light. I asked him why he didn't secure board with his cousin, the tin-pedler, but that made him angry, and he walked away in disgust. But I can't help pitying you a little, Harry."

"Why? On account of my occupation?"

"Partly. All these warm summer days, you have got to be working at the case, while I can lounge in the shade, or travel for pleasure. Sha'n't you have a vacation?"

"I don't expect any. I don't think I could well be spared. However, I don't mind it. I hope to do good deal of studying while you are gone."

"And I sha'n't do any."

"Neither would I, perhaps, in your position. But there's a good deal of difference between us. You are a Latin and Greek scholar, and can talk French, while I am at the bottom of the ladder. I have no time to lose."

"You have begun to mount the ladder, Harry. Don't be discouraged. You can climb up."
"But I must work for it. I haven't got high enough up to stop and rest. But there is one question I want to ask you, before you go."

"What is it?"

"What French book would you recommend after I have finished this Reader? I am nearly through now."
"Telemaque will be a good book to take next. It is easy and interesting. Have you got a French dictionary?"

"No; but I can buy one."

"You can use mine while I am gone. You may as well have it as not. I have no copy of Telemaque, but I will send you one from Boston."
"Agreed, provided you will let me pay you for it."

"So I would, if I had to buy one. But I have got an old copy, not very ornamental, but complete. I will send it through the mail."

"Thank you, Oscar. How kind you are!"

"Don't flatter me, Harry. The favors you refer to are but trifles. I will ask a favor of you in return."
"I wish you would."

"Then help me pack my trunk. There's nothing I detest so much. Generally I tumble things in helter-skelter, and get a good scolding from mother for doing it, when she inspects my trunk."

"I'll save you the trouble, then. Bring what you want to carry home, and pile it on the floor, and I'll do the packing."

"A thousand thanks, as the French say. It takes a load off my mind. By the way, here's a lot of my photographs. Would you like one to remember your professor by?"

"Very much, Oscar."

"Then take your choice. They don't do justice to my beauty, which is of a stunning description, as you are aware, nor do they convey an idea of the lofty intellect which sits enthroned behind my classic brow; but such as they are, you are welcome to one."

"Any one would think, to hear you, that you had no end of self-conceit, Oscar," said Harry, laughing.

"How do you know that I haven't? Most people think they are beautiful. A photographer told my sister that he was once visited by a frightfully homely man from the the country, who wanted his 'picter took.' When the result was placed before him, he seemed dissatisfied. 'Don't you think it like?' said the artist.—'Well, ye-es,' he answered slowly, 'but it hasn't got my sweet expression about the mouth!'"

"Very good," said Harry, laughing; "that's what's the matter with your picture."

"Precisely. I am glad your artistic eye detects what is wanting.
But, hold! there's a knock. It's Fitz, I'll bet a hat."
"Come in!" he cried, and Fletcher walked in.

"Good-evening, Fletcher," said Oscar. "You see I'm packing, or rather Walton is packing. He's a capital packer."

"Indeed!" sneered Fletcher. "I was not aware that Mr. Walton was in that line of business. What are his terms?"

"I refer you to him."

"What do you charge for packing trunks, Mr. Walton?"

"I think fifty cents would be about right," answered Harry, with perfect gravity. "Can you give me a job, Mr. Fletcher?"

"I might, if I had known it in time, though I am particular who handles my things."

"Walton is careful, and I can vouch for his honesty," said Oscar, carrying out the joke. "His wages in the printing office are not large, and he would be glad to make a little extra money."

"It must be very inconvenient to be poor," said Fletcher, with a supercilious glance at our hero, who was kneeling before Oscar's trunk.

"It is," answered Harry, quietly, "but as long as work is to be had I shall not complain."

"To be sure!" said Fletcher. "My father is wealthy, and I shall not have to work."

"Suppose he should fail?" suggested Oscar.

"That is a very improbable supposition," said Fletcher, loftily.

"But not impossible?"

"Nothing is impossible."

"Of course. I say, Fitz, if such a thing should happen, you've got something to fall back upon."

"To what do you refer?"

"Mr. Bickford could give you an interest in the tin business."

"Good-evening!" said Fletcher, not relishing the allusion.

"Good-evening! Of course I shall see you in the city."

"I suppose I ought not to tease Fitz," said Oscar, after his visitor had departed, "but I enjoy seeing how disgusted he looks."

In due time the trunk was packed, and Harry, not without regret, took leave of his friend for the summer.

CHAPTER XIV.

HARRY BECOMES AN AUTHOR.

The closing of the Academy made quite a difference in the life of Centreville. The number of boarding scholars was about thirty, and these, though few in number, were often seen in the street and at the postoffice, and their withdrawal left a vacancy. Harry Walton felt quite lonely at first; but there is no cure for loneliness like occupation, and he had plenty of that. The greater part of the day was spent in the printing office, while his evenings and early mornings were occupied in study and reading. He had become very much interested in French, in which he found himself advancing rapidly. Occasionally he took tea at Mr. Ferguson's, and this he always enjoyed; for, as I have already said, he and Ferguson held very similar views on many important subjects. One evening, at the house of the latter, he saw a file of weekly papers, which proved, on examination, to be back numbers of the "Weekly Standard," a literary paper issued in Boston.

"I take the paper for my family," said Ferguson. "It contains quite a variety of reading matter, stories, sketches and essays."

"It seems quite interesting," said Harry.

"Yes, it is. I will lend you some of the back numbers, if you like."

"I would like it. My father never took a literary paper; his means were so limited that he could not afford it."

"I think it is a good investment. There are few papers from which you cannot obtain in a year more than the worth of the subscription. Besides, if you are going to be an editor, it will be useful for you to become familiar with the manner in which such papers are conducted."

When Harry went home he took a dozen copies of the paper, and sat up late reading them. While thus engaged an idea struck him. It was this: Could not he write something which would be accepted for publication in the "Standard"? It was his great ambition to learn to write for the press, and he felt that he was old enough to commence.

"If I don't succeed the first time, I can try again," he reflected.

The more he thought of it, the more he liked the plan. It is very possible that he was influenced by the example of Franklin, who, while yet a boy in his teens, contributed articles to his brother's paper though at the time the authorship was not suspected. Finally he decided to commence writing as soon as he could think of a suitable subject. This he found was not easy. He could think of plenty of subjects of which he was not qualified to write, or in which he felt little interest; but he rightly decided that he could succeed better with something that had a bearing upon his own experience or hopes for the future.

Finally he decided to write on Ambition.

I do not propose to introduce Harry's essay in these pages, but will give a general idea of it, as tending to show his views of life.

He began by defining ambition as a desire for superiority, by which most men were more or less affected, though it manifested itself in very different ways, according to the character of him with whom it was found. Here I will quote a passage, as a specimen of Harry's style and mode of expression.

"There are some who denounce ambition as wholly bad and to be avoided by all; but I think we ought to make a distinction between true and false ambition. The desire of superiority is an honorable motive, if it leads to honorable exertion. I will mention Napoleon as an illustration of false ambition, which is selfish in itself, and has brought misery and ruin, to prosperous nations. Again, there are some who are ambitious to dress better than their neighbors, and their principal thoughts are centred upon the tie of their cravat, or the cut of their coat, if young men; or upon the richness and style of their dresses, if they belong to the other sex. Beau Brummel is a noted instance of this kind of ambition. It is said that fully half of his time was devoted to his toilet, and the other half to displaying it in the streets, or in society. Now this is a very low form of ambition, and it is wrong to indulge it, because it is a waste of time which could be much better employed."

Harry now proceeded to describe what he regarded as a true and praiseworthy ambition. He defined it as a desire to excel in what would be of service to the human race, and he instanced his old Franklin, who, induced by an honorable ambition, worked his way up to a high civil station, as well as a commanding position in the scientific world. He mentioned Columbus as ambitious to extend the limits of geographical knowledge, and made a brief reference to the difficulties and discouragements over which he triumphed on the way to success. He closed by an appeal to boys and young men to direct their ambition into worthy channels, so that even if they could not leave behind a great name, they might at least lead useful lives, and in dying have the satisfaction of thinking that they done some service to the race.

This will give a very fair idea of Harry's essay. There was nothing remarkable about it, and no striking originality in the ideas, but it was very creditably expressed for a boy of his years, and did even more credit to his good judgment, since it was an unfolding of the principles by which he meant to guide his own life.

It must not be supposed that our hero was a genius, and that he wrote his essay without difficulty. It occupied him two evenings to write it, and he employed the third in revising and copying it. It covered about five pages of manuscript, and, according to his estimate, would fill about two-thirds of a long column in the "Standard."

After preparing it, the next thing was to find a nom de plume, for he shrank from signing his own name. After long consideration, he at last decided upon Franklin, and this was the name he signed to his maiden contribution to the press.

He carried it to the post-office one afternoon, after his work in the printing office was over, and dropped it unobserved into the letter-box. He did not want the postmaster to learn his secret, as he would have done had he received it directly from him, and noted the address on the envelope.

For the rest of the week, Harry went about his work weighed down with his important secret—a secret which he had not even shared with Ferguson. If the essay was declined, as he thought it might very possibly be, he did not want any one to know it. If it were accepted, and printed, it would be time enough then to make it known. But there were few minutes in which his mind was not on his literary venture. His preoccupation was observed by his fellow-workmen in the office, and he was rallied upon it, good-naturedly, by Ferguson, but in a different spirit by Clapp.

"It seems to me you are unusually silent, Harry," said Ferguson.
"You're not in love, are you?"
"Not that I know of," said Harry, smiling. "It's rather too early yet."

"I've known boys of your age to fancy themselves in love."

"He is is more likely thinking up some great discovery," said Clapp, sneering. "You know he's a second Franklin."

"Thank you for the compliment," said our hero, good-humoredly, "but I don't deserve it. I don't expect to make any great discovery at present."

"I suppose you expect to set the river on fire, some day," said
Clapp, sarcastically.
"I am afraid it wouldn't do much good to try," said Harry, who was too sensible to take offence. "It isn't so easily done."

"I suppose some day we shall be proud of having been in the same office with so great a man," pursued Clapp.

"Really, Clapp, you're rather hard on our young friend," said Ferguson. "He doesn't put on any airs of superiority, or pretend to anything uncommon."

"He's very kind—such an intellect as he's got, too!" said Clapp.

"I'm glad you found it out," said Harry. "I haven't a very high idea of my intellect yet. I wish I had more reason to do so."

Finding that he had failed in his attempt to provoke Harry by his ridicule, Clapp desisted, but he disliked him none the less.

The fact was, that Clapp was getting into a bad way. He had no high aim in life, and cared chiefly for the pleasure of the present moment. He had found Luke Harrison a congenial companion, and they had been associated in more than one excess. The morning previous, Clapp had entered the printing office so evidently under the influence of liquor, that he had been sharply reprimanded by Mr. Anderson.

"I don't choose to interfere with your mode of life, unwise and ruinous as I may consider it," he said, "as long as it does not interfere with your discharge of duty. But to-day you are clearly incapacitated for labor, and I have a right to complain. If it happens again, I shall be obliged to look for another journeyman."

Clapp did not care to leave his place just at present, for he had no money saved up, and was even somewhat in debt, and it might be some time before he got another place. So he rather sullenly agreed to be more careful in future, and did not go to work till the afternoon. But though circumstances compelled him to submit, it put him in bad humor, and made him more disposed to sneer than ever. He had an unreasoning prejudice against Harry, which was stimulated by Luke Harrison, who had this very sufficient reason for hating our hero, that he had succeeded in injuring him. As an old proverb has it "We are slow to forgive those whom we have injured."

CHAPTER XV.

A LITERARY DEBUT.

Harry waited eagerly for the next issue of the "Weekly Standard." It was received by Mr. Anderson in exchange for the "Centreville Gazette," and usually came to hand on Saturday morning. Harry was likely to obtain the first chance of examining the paper, as he was ordinarily sent to the post-office on the arrival of the morning mail.

His hands trembled as he unfolded the paper and hurriedly scanned the contents. But he looked in vain for his essay on Ambition. There was not even a reference to it. He was disappointed, but he soon became hopeful again.

"I couldn't expect it to appear so soon," he reflected. "These city weeklies have to be printed some days in advance. It may appear yet."

So he was left in suspense another week, hopeful and doubtful by turns of the success of his first offering for the press. He was rallied from time to time on his silence in the office, but he continued to keep his secret. If his contribution was slighted, no one should know it but himself.

At last another Saturday morning came around and again he set out for the post-office. Again he opened the paper with trembling fingers, and eagerly scanned the well-filled columns. This time his search was rewarded. There, on the first column of the last page, in all the glory of print, was his treasured essay!

A flash of pleasure tinged his cheek, and his heart beat rapidly, as he read his first printed production. It is a great event in the life of a literary novice, when he first sees himself. Even Byron says,—

"'Tis pleasant, sure, to see one's self in print."

To our young hero the essay read remarkably well—better than he had expected; but then, very likely he was prejudiced in its favor. He read it through three times on his way back to the printing office, and each time felt better satisfied.

"I wonder if any of the readers will think it was written by a boy?" thought Harry. Probably many did so suspect, for, as I have said, though the thoughts were good and sensible, the article was only moderately well expressed. A practised critic would readily have detected marks of immaturity, although it was a very creditable production for a boy of sixteen.

"Shall I tell Ferguson?" thought Harry.

On the whole he concluded to remain silent just at present. He knew Ferguson took the paper, and waited to see if he would make any remark about it.

"I should like to hear him speak of it, without knowing that I was the writer," thought our hero.

Just before he reached the office, he discovered with satisfaction the following editorial reference to his article:—

"We print in another column an essay on 'ambition' by a new contributor. It contains some good ideas, and we especially commend it to the perusal of our young readers. We hope to hear from 'Franklin' again."

"That's good," thought Harry. "I am glad the editor likes it. I shall write again as soon as possible."

"What makes you look so bright, Harry?" asked Ferguson, as he re-entered the office. "Has any one left you a fortune?"

"Not that I know of," said Harry. "Do I look happier than usual?"

"So it seems to me."

Harry was spared answering this question, for Clapp struck in, grumbling, as usual: "I wish somebody'd leave me a fortune. You wouldn't see me here long."

"What would you do?" asked his fellow-workman.

"Cut work to begin with. I'd go to Europe and have a jolly time."

"You can do that without a fortune."

"I should like to know how?"

"Be economical, and you can save enough in three years to pay for a short trip. Bayard Taylor was gone two years, and only spent five hundred dollars."

"Oh, hang economy!" drawled Clapp. "It don't suit me. I should like to know how a feller's going to economize on fifteen dollars a week."

"I could."

"Oh, no doubt," sneered Clapp, "but a man can't starve."

"Come round and take supper with me, some night," said Ferguson, good-humoredly, "and you can judge for yourself whether I believe in starving."

Clapp didn't reply to this invitation. He would not have enjoyed a quiet evening with his fellow-workman. An evening at billiards or cards, accompanied by bets on the games, would have been much more to his mind.

"Who is Bayard Taylor, that made such a cheap tour in Europe?" asked
Harry, soon afterward.
"A young journalist who had a great desire to travel. He has lately published an account of his tour. I don't buy many books, but I bought that. Would you like to read it?"

"Very much."

"You can have it any time."

"Thank you."

On Monday, a very agreeable surprise awaited Harry.

"I am out of copy," he said, going up to Mr. Anderson's table.

"Here's a selection for the first page," said Mr. Anderson. "Cut it in two, and give part of it to Clapp."

Could Harry believe his eyes! It was his own article on ambition, and it was to be reproduced in the "Gazette." Next to the delight of seeing one's self in print for the first time, is the delight of seeing that first article copied. It is a mark of appreciation which cannot be mistaken.

Still Harry said nothing, but, with a manner as unconcerned as possible, handed the lower half of the essay to Clapp to set up. The signature "Franklin" had been cut off, and the name of the paper from which the essay had been cut was substituted.

"Wouldn't Clapp feel disgusted," thought Harry, "if he knew that he was setting up an article of mine. I believe he would have a fit."

He was too considerate to expose his fellow-workman to such a contingency, and went about his work in silence.

That evening he wrote to the publisher of the "Standard," inclosing the price of two copies of the last number, which he desired should be sent to him by mail. He wished to keep one himself, and the other he intended to forward to his father, who, he knew, would sympathize with him in his success as well as his aspirations. He accompanied the paper by a letter in which he said,—

"I want to improve in writing as much as, I can. I want to be something more than a printer, sometime. I shall try to qualify myself for an editor; for an editor can exert a good deal of influence in the community. I hope you will approve my plans."

In due time Harry received the following reply:—

"My dear son:—I am indeed pleased and proud to hear of your success, not that it is a great matter in itself, but because I think it shows that you are in earnest in your determination to win an honorable position by honorable labor. I am sorry that my narrow means have not permitted me to give you those advantages which wealthy fathers can bestow upon their sons. I should like to have sent you to college and given you an opportunity afterward of studying for a profession. I think your natural abilities would have justified such an outlay. But, alas! poverty has always held me back. It shuts out you, as it has shut out me, from the chance of culture. Your college, my boy, must be the printing office. If you make the best of that, you will find that it is no mean instructor. Not Franklin alone, but many of our most eminent and influential men have graduated from it.

"You will be glad to hear that we are all well. I have sold the cow which I bought of Squire Green, and got another in her place that proves to be much better. We all send much love, and your mother wishes me to say that she misses you very much, as indeed we all do. But we know that you are better off in Centreville than you would be at home, and that helps to make us contented. Don't forget to write every week.

"Your affectionate father,
"HIRAM WALTON.
"P. S.—If you print any more articles, we shall be interested to read them."

Harry read this letter with eager interest. He felt glad that his father was pleased with him, and it stimulated him to increased exertions.

"Poor father!" he said to himself. "He has led a hard life, cultivating that rocky little farm. It has been hard work and poor pay with him. I hope there is something better in store for him. If I ever get rich, or even well off, I will take care that he has an easier time."

After the next issue of the "Gazette" had appeared, Harry informed Ferguson in confidence that he was the author of the article on Ambition.

"I congratulate you, Harry," said his friend. "It is an excellent essay, well thought out, and well expressed. I don't wonder, now you tell me of it. It sounds like you. Without knowing the authorship, I asked Clapp his opinion of it."

"What did he say?"

"Are you sure it won't hurt your feelings?"

"It may; but I shall get over it. Go ahead."

"He said it was rubbish."

Harry laughed.

"He would be confirmed in his decision, if he knew that I wrote it," he said.

"No doubt. But don't let that discourage you. Keep on writing by all means, and you'll become an editor in time."

CHAPTER XVI.

FERDINAND B. KENSINGTON.

It has already been mentioned that John Clapp and Luke Harrison were intimate. Though their occupations differed, one being a printer and the other a shoemaker, they had similar tastes, and took similar views of life. Both were discontented with the lot which Fortune had assigned them. To work at the case, or the shoe-bench, seemed equally irksome, and they often lamented to each other the hard necessity which compelled them to it. Suppose we listen to their conversation, as they walked up the village street, one evening about this time, smoking cigars.

"I say, Luke," said John Clapp, "I've got tired of this kind of life. Here I've been in the office a year, and I'm not a cent richer than when I entered it, besides working like a dog all the while."

"Just my case," said Luke. "I've been shoe-makin' ever since I was fourteen, and I'll be blest if I can show five dollars, to save my life."

"What's worse," said Clapp, "there isn't any prospect of anything better in my case. What's a feller to do on fifteen dollars a week?"

"Won't old Anderson raise your wages?"

"Not he! He thinks I ought to get rich on what he pays me now," and Clapp laughed scornfully. "If I were like Ferguson, I might. He never spends a cent without taking twenty-four hours to think it over beforehand."

My readers, who are familiar with Mr. Ferguson's views and ways of life, will at once see that this was unjust, but justice cannot be expected from an angry and discontented man.

"Just so," said Luke. "If a feller was to live on bread and water, and get along with one suit of clothes a year, he might save something, but that aint my style."

"Nor mine."

"It's strange how lucky some men are," said Luke. "They get rich without tryin'. I never was lucky. I bought a ticket in a lottery once, but of course I didn't draw anything. Just my luck!"

"So did I," said Clapp, "but I fared no better. It seemed as if Fortune had a spite against me. Here I am twenty-five years old, and all I'm worth is two dollars and a half, and I owe more than that to the tailor."

"You're as rich as I am," said Luke. "I only get fourteen dollars a week. That's less than you do."

"A dollar more or less don't amount to much," said Clapp. "I'll tell you what it is, Luke," he resumed after a pause, "I'm getting sick of Centreville."

"So am I," said Luke, "but it don't make much difference. If I had fifty dollars, I'd go off and try my luck somewhere else, but I'll have to wait till I'm gray-headed before I get as much as that."

"Can't you borrow it?"

"Who'd lend it to me?"

"I don't know. If I did, I'd go in for borrowing myself. I wish there was some way of my getting to California."

"California!" repeated Luke with interest. "What would you do there?"

"I'd go to the mines."

"Do you think there's money to be made there?"

"I know there is," said Clapp, emphatically.

"How do you know it?"

"There's an old school-mate of mine—Ralph Smith—went out there two years ago. Last week he returned home—I heard it in a letter—and how much do you think he brought with him?"

"How much?"

"Eight thousand dollars!"

"Eight thousand dollars! He didn't make it all at the mines, did he?"

"Yes, he did. When he went out there, he had just money enough to pay his passage. Now, after only two years, he can lay off and live like a gentleman."

"He's been lucky, and no mistake."

"You bet he has. But we might be as lucky if we were only out there."

"Ay, there's the rub. A fellow can't travel for nothing."

At this point in their conversation, a well-dressed young man, evidently a stranger in the village, met them, and stopping, asked politely for a light.

This Clapp afforded him.

"You are a stranger in the village?" he said, with some curiosity.

"Yes, I was never here before. I come from New York."

"Indeed! If I lived in New York I'd stay there, and not come to such a beastly place as Centreville."

"Do you live here?" asked the stranger.

"Yes."

"I wonder you live in such a beastly place," he said, with a smile.

"You wouldn't, if you knew the reason."

"What is the reason?"

"I can't get away."

The stranger laughed.

"Cruel parents?" he asked.

"Not much," said Clapp. "The plain reason is, that I haven't got money enough to get me out of town."

"It's the same with me," said Luke Harrison.

"Gentlemen, we are well met," said the stranger. "I'm hard up myself."

"You don't look like it," said Luke, glancing at his rather flashy attire.

"These clothes are not paid for," said the stranger, laughing; "and what's more, I don't think they are likely to be. But, I take it, you gentlemen are better off than I in one respect. You've got situations—something to do."

"Yes, but on starvation pay," said Clapp. "I'm in the office of the 'Centreville Gazette.'"

"And I'm in a shoemaker's shop. It's a beastly business for a young man of spirit," said Luke.

"Well, I'm a gentleman at large, living on my wits, and pretty poor living it is sometimes," said the stranger. "As I think we'll agree together pretty well, I'm glad I've met you. We ought to know each other better. There's my card."

He drew from his pocket a highly glazed piece of pasteboard, bearing the name,

FREDERICK B. KENSINGTON.

"I haven't any cards with me," said Clapp, "but my name is John Clapp."

"And mine is Luke Harrison," said the bearer of that appellation.

"I'm proud to know you, gentlemen. If you have no objection, we'll walk on together."

To this Clapp and Luke acceded readily. Indeed, they were rather proud of being seen in company with a young man so dashing in manner, and fashionably dressed, though in a pecuniary way their new acquaintance, by his own confession, was scarcely as well off as themselves.

"Where are you staying, Mr. Kensington?" said Clapp.

"At the hotel. It's a poor place. No style."

"Of course not. I can't help wondering, Mr. Kensington, what can bring you to such a one-horse place as this."

"I don't mind telling you, then. The fact is, I've got an old aunt living about two miles from here. She's alone in the world—got neither chick nor child—and is worth at least ten thousand dollars. Do you see?"

"I think I do," said Clapp. "You want to come in for a share of the stamps."

"Yes; I want to see if I can't get something out of the old girl," said Kensington, carelessly.

"Do you think the chance is good?"

"I don't know. I hear she's pretty tight-fisted. But I've run on here on the chance of doing something. If she will only make me her heir, and give me five hundred dollars in hand, I'll go to California, and see what'll turn up."

"California!" repeated John Clapp and Luke in unison.

"Yes; were you ever there?"

"No; but we were talking of going there just as you came up," said John. "An old school-mate of mine has just returned from there with eight thousand dollars in gold."

"Lucky fellow! That's the kind of haul I'd like to make."

"Do you know how much it costs to go out there?"

"The prices are down just at present. You can go for a hundred dollars—second cabin."

"It might as well be a thousand!" said Luke. "Clapp and I can't raise a hundred dollars apiece to save our lives."

"I'll tell you what," said Kensington. "You two fellows are just the company I'd like. If I can raise five hundred dollars out of the old girl, I'll take you along with me, and you can pay me after you get out there."

John Clapp and Luke Harrison were astounded at this liberal offer from a perfect stranger, but they had no motives of delicacy about accepting it. They grasped the hand of their new friend, and assured him that nothing would suit them so well.

"All right!" said Kensington. "Then it's agreed. Now, boys, suppose we go round to the tavern, and ratify our compact by a drink."

"I say amen to that," answered Clapp, "but I insist on standing treat."

"Just as you say," said Kensington. "Come along."

It was late when the three parted company. Luke and John Clapp were delighted with their new friend, and, as they staggered home with uncertain steps, they indulged in bright visions of future prosperity.

CHAPTER XVII.

AUNT DEBORAH.

Miss Deborah Kensington sat in an old-fashioned rocking-chair covered with a cheap print, industriously engaged in footing a stocking. She was a maiden lady of about sixty, with a thin face, thick seamed with wrinkles, a prominent nose, bridged by spectacles, sharp gray eyes, and thin lips. She was a shrewd New England woman, who knew very well how to take care of and increase the property which she had inherited. Her nephew had been correctly informed as to her being close-fisted. All her establishment was carried on with due regard to economy, and though her income in the eyes of a city man would be counted small, she saved half of it every year, thus increasing her accumulations.

As she sat placidly knitting, an interruption came in the shape of a knock at the front door.

"I'll go myself," she said, rising, and laying down the stocking. "Hannah's out in the back room, and won't hear. I hope it aint Mrs. Smith, come to borrow some butter. She aint returned that last half-pound she borrowed. She seems to think her neighbors have got to support her."

These thoughts were in her mind as she opened the door. But no Mrs. Smith presented her figure to the old lady's gaze. She saw instead, with considerable surprise, a stylish young man with a book under his arm. She jumped to the conclusion that he was a book-pedler, having been annoyed by several persistent specimens of that class of travelling merchants.

"If you've got books to sell," she said, opening the attack, "you may as well go away. I aint got no money to throw away."

Mr. Ferdinand B. Kensington—for he was the young man in question—laughed heartily, while the old lady stared at him half amazed, half angry.

"I don't see what there is to laugh at," said she, offended.

"I was laughing at the idea of my being taken for a book-pedler."

"Well, aint you one?" she retorted. "If you aint, what be you?"

"Aunt Deborah, don't you know me?" asked the young man, familiarly.

"Who are you that calls me aunt?" demanded the old lady, puzzled.

"I'm your brother Henry's son. My name is Ferdinand."

"You don't say so!" ejaculated the old lady. "Why, I'd never 'ave thought it. I aint seen you since you was a little boy."

"This don't look as if I was a little boy, aunt," said the young man, touching his luxuriant whiskers.

"How time passes, I do declare!" said Deborah. "Well, come in, and we'll talk over old times. Where did you come from?"

"From the city of New York. That's where I've been living for some time."

"You don't say! Well, what brings you this way?"

"To see you, Aunt Deborah. It's so long since I've seen you that I thought I'd like to come."

"I'm glad to see you, Ferdinand," said the old lady, flattered by such a degree of dutiful attention from a fine-looking young man. "So your poor father's dead?"

"Yes, aunt, he's been dead three years."

"I suppose he didn't leave much. He wasn't very forehanded."

"No, aunt; he left next to nothing."

"Well, it didn't matter much, seein' as you was the only child, and big enough to take care of yourself."

"Still, aunt, it would have been comfortable if he had left me a few thousand dollars."

"Aint you doin' well? You look as if you was," said Deborah, surveying critically her nephew's good clothes.

"Well, I've been earning a fair salary, but it's very expensive living in a great city like New York."

"Humph! that's accordin' as you manage. If you live snug, you can get along there cheap as well as anywhere, I reckon. What was you doin'?"

"I was a salesman for A. T. Stewart, our leading dry-goods merchant."

"What pay did you get?"

"A thousand dollars a year."

"Why, that's a fine salary. You'd ought to save up a good deal."

"You don't realize how much it costs to live in New York, aunt. Of course, if I lived here, I could live on half the sum, but I have to pay high prices for everything in New York."

"You don't need to spend such a sight on dress," said Deborah, disapprovingly.

"I beg your pardon, Aunt Deborah; that's where you are mistaken. The store-keepers in New York expect you to dress tip-top and look genteel, so as to do credit to them. If it hadn't been for that, I shouldn't have spent half so much for dress. Then, board's very expensive."

"You can get boarded here for two dollars and a half a week," said
Aunt Deborah.
"Two dollars and a half! Why, I never paid less than eight dollars a week in the city, and you can only get poor board for that."

"The boarding-houses must make a great deal of money," said Deborah.
"If I was younger, I'd maybe go to New York, and keep one myself."
"You're rich, aunt. You don't need to do that."

"Who told you I was rich?" said the old lady, quickly.

"Why, you've only got yourself to take care of, and you own this farm, don't you?"

"Yes, but farmin' don't pay much."

"I always heard you were pretty comfortable."

"So I am," said the old lady, "and maybe I save something; but my income aint as great as yours."

"You have only yourself to look after, and it is cheap living in
Centreville."
"I don't fling money away. I don't spend quarter as much as you on dress."

Looking at the old lady'a faded bombazine dress, Ferdinand was very ready to believe this.

"You don't have to dress here, I suppose," he answered. "But, aunt, we won't talk about money matters just yet. It was funny you took me for a book-pedler."

"It was that book you had, that made me think so."

"It's a book I brought as a present to you, Aunt Deborah."

"You don't say!" said the old lady, gratified. "What is it? Let me look at it."

"It's a copy of 'Pilgrim's Progress,' illustrated. I knew you wouldn't like the trashy books they write nowadays, so I brought you this."

"Really, Ferdinand, you're very considerate," said Aunt Deborah, turning over the leaves with manifest pleasure. "It's a good book, and I shall be glad to have it. Where are you stoppin'?"

"At the hotel in the village."

"You must come and stay here. You can get 'em to send round your things any time."

"Thank you, aunt, I shall be delighted to do so. It seems so pleasant to see you again after so many years. You don't look any older than when I saw you last."

Miss Deborah knew very well that she did look older, but still she was pleased by the compliment. Is there any one who does not like to receive the same assurance?

"I'm afraid your eyes aint very sharp, Ferdinand," she said. "I feel
I'm gettin' old. Why, I'm sixty-one, come October."
"Are you? I shouldn't call you over fifty, from your looks, aunt.
Really I shouldn't."
"I'm afraid you tell fibs sometimes," said Aunt Deborah, but she said it very graciously, and surveyed her nephew very kindly. "Heigh ho! it's a good while since your poor father and I were children together, and went to the school-house on the hill. Now he's gone, and I'm left alone."

"Not alone, aunt. If he is dead, you have got a nephew."

"Well, Ferdinand, I'm glad to see you, and I shall be glad to have you pay me a good long visit. But how can you be away from your place so long? Did Mr. Stewart give you a vacation?"

"No, aunt; I left him."

"For good?"

"Yes."

"Left a place where you was gettin' a thousand dollars a year!" said the old lady in accents of strong disapproval.

"Yes, aunt."

"Then I think you was very foolish," said Deborah with emphasis.

"Perhaps you won't, when you know why I left it."

"Why did you?"

"Because I could do better."

"Better than a thousand dollars a year!" said Deborah with surprise.

"Yes, I am offered two thousand dollars in San Francisco."

"You don't say!" ejaculated Deborah, letting her stocking drop in sheer amazement.

"Yes, I do. It's a positive fact."

"You must be a smart clerk!"

"Well, it isn't for me to say," said Ferdinand, laughing.

"When be you goin' out?"

"In a week, but I thought I must come and bid you good-by first."

"I'm real glad to see you, Ferdinand," said Aunt Deborah, the more warmly because she considered him so prosperous that she would have no call to help him. But here she was destined to find herself mistaken.

CHAPTER XVIII.

AUNT AND NEPHEW.

"I don't think I can come here till to-morrow, Aunt Deborah," said Ferdinand, a little later. "I'll stay at the hotel to-night, and come round with my baggage in the morning."

"Very well, nephew, but now you're here, you must stay to tea."

"Thank you, aunt, I will."

"I little thought this mornin', I should have Henry's son to tea," said Aunt Deborah, half to herself. "You don't look any like him, Ferdinand."

"No, I don't think I do."

"It's curis too, for you was his very picter when you was a boy."

"I've changed a good deal since then, Aunt Deborah," said her nephew, a little uneasily.

"So you have, to be sure. Now there's your hair used to be almost black, now it's brown. Really I can't account for it," and Aunt Deborah surveyed the young man over her spectacles.

"You've got a good memory, aunt," said Ferdinand with a forced laugh.

"Now ef your hair had grown darker, I shouldn't have wondered," pursued Aunt Deborah; "but it aint often black turns to brown."

"That's so, aunt, but I can explain it," said Ferdinand, after a slight pause.

"How was it?"

"You know the French barbers can change your hair to any shade you want."

"Can they?"

"Yes, to be sure. Now—don't laugh at me, aunt—a young lady I used to like didn't fancy dark hair, so I went to a French barber, and he changed the color for me in three months."

"You don't say!"

"Fact, aunt; but he made me pay him well too."

"How much did you give him?"

"Fifty dollars, aunt."

"That's what I call wasteful," said Aunt Deborah, disapprovingly.

"Couldn't you be satisfied with the nat'ral color of your hair? To my mind black's handsomer than brown."

"You're right, aunt. I wouldn't have done it if it hadn't been for
Miss Percival."
"Are you engaged to her?"

"No, Aunt Deborah. The fact was, I found she wasn't domestic, and didn't know anything about keeping house, but only cared for dress, so I drew off, and she's married to somebody else now."

"I'm glad to hear it," said Deborah, emphatically. "The jade! She wouldn't have been a proper wife for you. You want some good girl that's willin' to go into the kitchen, and look after things, and not carry all she's worth on her back."

"I agree with you, aunt," said Ferdinand, who thought it politic, in view of the request he meant to make by and by, to agree with hie aunt in her views of what a wife should be.

Aunt Deborah began to regard her nephew as quite a sensible young man, and to look upon him with complacency.

"I wish, Ferdinand," she said, "you liked farmin'."

"Why, aunt?"

"You could stay here, and manage my farm for me."

"Heaven forbid!" thought the young man with a shudder. "I should be bored to death. Does the old lady think I would put on a frock and overalls, and go out and plough, or hoe potatoes?"

"It's a good, healthy business," pursued Aunt Deborah, unconscious of the thoughts which were passing through her nephew's mind, "and you wouldn't have to spend much for dress. Then I'm gittin' old, and though I don't want to make no promises, I'd very likely will it to you, ef I was satisfied with the way you managed."

"You're very kind, aunt," said Ferdinand, "but I'm afraid I wasn't cut out for farming. You know I never lived in the country."

"Why, yes, you did," said the old lady. "You was born in the country, and lived there till you was ten years old."

"To be sure," said Ferdinand, hastily, "but I was too young then to take notice of farming. What does a boy of ten know of such things?"

"To be sure. You're right there."

"The fact is, Aunt Deborah, some men are born to be farmers, and some are born to be traders. Now, I've got a talent for trading. That's the reason I've got such a good offer from San Francisco."

"How did you get it? Did you know the man?"

"He used to be in business in New York. He was the first man I worked for, and he knew what I was. San Francisco is full of money, and traders make more than they do here. That's the reason he can afford to offer me so large a salary."

"When did he send for you?"

"I got the letter last week."

"Have you got it with you?"

"No, aunt; I may have it at the hotel," said the young man, hesitating, "but I am not certain."

"Well, it's a good offer. There isn't nobody in Centreville gets so large a salary."

"No, I suppose not. They don't need it, as it is cheap living here."

"I hope when you get out there, Ferdinand, you'll save up money.
You'd ought to save two-thirds of your pay."
"I will try to, aunt."

"You'll be wantin' to get married bimeby, and then it'll be convenient to have some money to begin with."

"To be sure, aunt. I see you know how to manage."

"I was always considered a good manager," said Deborah, complacently. "Ef your poor father had had my faculty, he wouldn't have died as poor as he did, I can tell you."

"What a conceited old woman she is, with her faculty!" thought
Ferdinand, but what he said was quite different.
"I wish he had had, aunt. It would have been better for me."

"Well, you ought to get along, with your prospects."

"Little the old woman knows what my real prospects are!" thought the young man.

"Of course I ought," he said.

"Excuse me a few minutes, nephew," said Aunt Deborah, gathering up her knitting and rising from her chair. "I must go out and see about tea. Maybe you'd like to read that nice book you brought."

"No, I thank you, aunt. I think I'll take a little walk round your place, if you'll allow me."

"Sartin, Ferdinand. Only come back in half an hour; tea'll be ready then."

"Yea, aunt, I'll remember."

So while Deborah was in the kitchen, Ferdinand took a walk in the fields, laughing to himself from time to time, as if something amused him.

He returned in due time, and sat down to supper Aunt Deborah had provided her best, and, though the dishes were plain, they were quite palatable.

When supper was over, the young man said,—

"Now, aunt, I think I will be getting back to the hotel."

"You'll come over in the morning, Ferdinand, and fetch your trunk?"

"Yes, aunt. Good-night."

"Good-night."

"Well," thought the young man, as he tramped back to the hotel. "I've opened the campaign, and made, I believe, a favorable impression. But what a pack of lies I have had to tell, to be sure! The old lady came near catching me once or twice, particularly about the color of my hair. It was a lucky thought, that about the French barber. It deceived the poor old soul. I don't think she could ever have been very handsome. If she was she must have changed fearfully."

In the evening, John Clapp and Luke Harrison came round to the hotel to see him.

"Have you been to see your aunt?" asked Clapp.

"Yes, I took tea there."

"Have a good time?"

"Oh, I played the dutiful nephew to perfection. The old lady thinks a sight of me."

"How did you do it?"

"I agreed with all she said, told her how young she looked, and humbugged her generally."

Clapp laughed.

"The best part of the joke is—will you promise to keep dark?"

"Of course."

"Don't breathe it to a living soul, you two fellows. She isn't my aunt of all!"

"Isn't your aunt?"

"No, her true nephew is in New York—I know him.—but I know enough of family matters to gull the old lady, and, I hope, raise a few hundred dollars out of her."

This was a joke which Luke and Clapp could appreciate, and they laughed heartily at the deception which was being practised on simple Aunt Deborah, particularly when Ferdinand explained how he got over the difficulty of having different colored hair from the real owner of the name he assumed.

"We must have a drink on that," said Luke. "Walk up, gentlemen."

"I'm agreeable," said Ferdinand.

"And I," said Clapp. "Never refuse a good offer, say I."

Poor Aunt Deborah! She little dreamed that she was the dupe of a designing adventurer who bore no relationship to her.

CHAPTER XIX.

THE ROMANCE OF A RING.

Ferdinand B. Kensington, as he called himself, removed the next morning to the house of Aunt Deborah. The latter received him very cordially, partly because it was a pleasant relief to her solitude to have a lively and active young man in the house, partly because she was not forced to look upon him as a poor relation in need of pecuniary assistance. She even felt considerable respect for the prospective recipient of an income of two thousand dollars, which in her eyes was a magnificent salary.

Ferdinand, on his part, spared no pains to make himself agreeable to the old lady, whom he had a mercenary object in pleasing. Finding that she was curious to hear about the great city, which to her was as unknown as London or Paris, be gratified her by long accounts, chiefly of as imaginative character, to which she listened greedily. These included some personal adventures, in all of which he figured very creditably.

Here is a specimen.

"By the way, Aunt Deborah," he said, casually, "have you noticed this ring on my middle finger?"

"No, I didn't notice it before, Ferdinand. It's very handsome."

"I should think it ought to be, Aunt Deborah," said the young man.

"Why?"

"It cost enough to be handsome."

"How much did it cost?" asked the old lady, not without curiosity.

"Guess."

"I aint no judge of such things; I've only got this plain gold ring. Yours has got some sort of a stone in it."
"That stone is a diamond, Aunt Deborah!"

"You don't say so! Let me look at it. It aint got no color. Looks like glass."

"It's very expensive, though. How much do you think it cost?"

"Well, maybe five dollars."

"Five dollars!" ejaculated the young man. "Why, what can you be thinking of, Aunt Deborah?"

"I shouldn't have guessed so much," said the old lady, misunderstanding him, "only you said it was expensive."

"So it is. Five dollars would be nothing at all."

"You don't say it cost more?"

"A great deal more."

"Did it cost ten dollars?"

"More."

"Fifteen?"

"I see, aunt, you have no idea of the cost of diamond rings! You may believe me or not, but that ring cost six hundred and fifty dollars."

"What!" almost screamed Aunt Deborah, letting fall her knitting in her surprise.

"It's true."

"Six hundred and fifty dollars for a little piece of gold and glass!" ejaculated the old lady.

"Diamond, aunt, not glass."

"Well, it don't look a bit better'n glass, and I do say," proceeded Deborah, with energy, "that it's a sin and a shame to pay so much money for a ring. Why, it was more than half your year's salary, Ferdinand."
"I agree with you, aunt; it would have been very foolish and wrong for a young man on a small salary like mine to buy so expensive a ring as this. I hope, Aunt Deborah, I have inherited too much of your good sense to do that."

"Then where did you get it?" asked the old lady, moderating her tone.

"It was given to me."

"Given to you! Who would give you such a costly present?"

"A rich man whose life I once saved, Aunt Deborah."

"You don't say so, Ferdinand!" said Aunt Deborah, interested. "Tell me all about it."

"So I will, aunt, though I don't often speak of it," said Ferdinand, modestly. "It seems like boasting, you know, and I never like to do that. But this is the way it happened.

"Now for a good tough lie!" said Ferdinand to himself, as the old lady suspended her work, and bent forward with eager attention.

"You know, of course, that New York and Brooklyn are on opposite sides of the river, and that people have to go across in ferry-boats."

"Yes, I've heard that, Ferdinand."

"I'm glad of that, because now you'll know that my story is correct. Well, one summer I boarded over in Brooklyn—on the Heights—and used to cross the ferry morning and night. It was the Wall street ferry, and a great many bankers and rich merchants used to cross daily also. One of these was a Mr. Clayton, a wholesale dry-goods merchant, immensely rich, whom I knew by sight, though I had never spoken to him. It was one Thursday morning—I remember even the day of the week—when the boat was unusually full. Mr. Clayton was leaning against the side-railing talking to a friend, when all at once the railing gave way, and he fell backward into the water, which immediately swallowed him up."

"Merciful man!" ejaculated Aunt Deborah, intensely interested. "Go on, Ferdinand."

"Of course there was a scene of confusion and excitement," continued Ferdinand, dramatically. 'Man overboard! Who will save him?' said more than one. 'I will,' I exclaimed, and in an instant I had sprang over the railing into the boiling current."

"Weren't you frightened to death?" asked the old lady. "Could you swim?"

"Of course I could. More than once I have swum all the way from New York to Brooklyn. I caught Mr. Clayton by the collar, as he was sinking for the third time, and shouted to a boatman near by to come to my help. Well, there isn't much more to tell. We were taken on board the boat, and rowed to shore. Mr. Clayton recovered his senses so far as to realize that I had saved his life.

"'What is your name, young man?' he asked, grasping my hand.

"'Ferdinand B. Kensington,' I answered modestly.

"'You have saved my life,' he said warmly.

"'I am very glad of it,' said I.

"'You have shown wonderful bravery."

"'Oh no,' I answered. 'I know how to swim, and I wasn't going to see you drown before my eyes.'

"'I shall never cease to be grateful to you.'

"'Oh, don't think of it,' said I.

"'But I must think of it,' he answered. 'But for you I should now be a senseless corpse lying in the bottom of the river,' and he shuddered.

"'Mr. Clayton,' said I, 'let me advise you to get home as soon as possible, or you will catch your death of cold.'

"'So will you,' he said. 'You must come with me.'

"He insisted, so I went, and was handsomely treated, you may depend. Mr. Clayton gave me a new suit of clothes, and the next morning he took me to Tiffany's—that's the best jeweller in New York—and bought me this diamond ring. He first offered me money, but I felt delicate about taking money for such a service, and told him so. So he bought me this ring."

"Well, I declare!" ejaculated Aunt Deborah.

"That was an adventure. But it seems to me, Ferdinand, I would have taken the money."

"As to that, aunt, I can sell this ring, if ever I get hard up, but I hope I sha'n't be obliged to."

"You certainly behaved very well, Ferdinand. Do you ever see Mr. Clayton now?"
"Sometimes, but I don't seek his society, for fear he would think I wanted to get something more out of him."

"How much money do you think he'd have given you?" asked Aunt Deborah, who was of a practical nature.
"A thousand dollars, perhaps more."

"Seems to me I would have taken it."

"If I had, people would have said that's why I jumped into the water, whereas I wasn't thinking anything about getting a reward. So now, aunt, you won't think it very strange that I wear such an expensive ring."

"Of course it makes a difference, as you didn't buy it yourself. I don't see how folks can be such fools as to throw away hundreds of dollars for such a trifle."

"Well, aunt, everybody isn't as sensible and practical as you. Now I agree with you; I think it's very foolish. Still I'm glad I've got the ring, because I can turn it into money when I need to. Only, you see, I don't like to part with a gift, although I don't think Mr. Clayton would blame me."

"Of course he wouldn't, Ferdinand. But I don't see why you should need money when you're goin' to get such a handsome salary in San Francisco."

"To be sure, aunt, but there's something else. However, I won't speak of it to-day. To-morrow I may want to ask your advice on a matter of business."

"I'll advise you the best I can, Ferdinand," said the flattered spinster.

"You see, aunt, you're so clear-headed, I shall place great dependence on your advice. But I think I'll take a little walk now, just to stretch my limbs."

"I've made good progress," said the young man to himself, as he lounged over the farm. "The old lady swallows it all. To-morrow must come my grand stroke. I thought I wouldn't propose it to-day, for fear she'd suspect the ring story."

CHAPTER XX.

A BUSINESS TRANSACTION.

Ferdinand found life at the farm-house rather slow, nor did he particularly enjoy the society of the spinster whom he called aunt. But he was playing for a valuable stake, and meant to play out his game.

"Strike while the iron is hot!" said he to himself; "That's a good rule; but how shall I know when it is hot? However, I must risk something, and take my chances with the old lady."

Aunt Deborah herself hastened his action. Her curiosity had been aroused by Ferdinand's intimation that he wished her advice on a matter of business, and the next morning, after breakfast, she said, "Ferdinand, what was that you wanted to consult me about? You may as well tell me now as any time."

"Here goes, then!" thought the young man.

"I'll tell you, aunt. You know I am offered a large salary in San Francisco?"
"Yes, you told me so."

"And, as you said the other day, I can lay up half my salary, and in time become a rich man."

"To be sure you can."

"But there is one difficulty in the way."

"What is that?"

"I must go out there."

"Of course you must," said the old lady, who did not yet see the point.

"And unfortunately it costs considerable money."

"Haven't you got enough money to pay your fare out there?"

"No, aunt; it is very expensive living in New York, and I was unable to save anything from my salary."

"How much does it cost to go out there?"

"About two hundred and fifty dollars."

"That's a good deal of money."

"So it is; but it will be a great deal better to pay it than to lose so good a place."

"I hope," said the old lady, sharply, "you don't expect me to pay your expenses out there."

"My dear aunt," said Ferdinand, hastily, "how can you suspect such a thing?"

"Then what do you propose to do?" asked the spinster, somewhat relieved.

"I wanted to ask your advice."

"Sell your ring. It's worth over six hundred dollars."

"Very true; but I should hardly like to part with it. I'll tell you what I have thought of. It cost six hundred and fifty dollars. I will give it as security to any one who will lend me five hundred dollars, with permission to sell it if I fail to pay up the note in six months. By the way, aunt, why can't you accommodate me in this matter? You will lose nothing, and I will pay handsome interest."

"How do you know I have the money?"

"I don't know; but I think you must have. But, although I am your nephew, I wouldn't think of asking you to lend me money without security. Business is business, so I say."

"Very true, Ferdinand."

"I ask nothing on the score of relationship, but I will make a business proposal."

"I don't believe the ring would fetch over six hundred dollars."

"It would bring just about that. The other fifty dollars represent the profit. Now, aunt, I'll make you a regular business proposal. If you'll lend me five hundred dollars, I'll give you my note for five hundred and fifty, bearing interest at six per cent., payable in six months, or, to make all sure, say in a year. I place the ring in your hands, with leave to sell it at the end of that time if I fail to carry out my agreement. But I sha'n't if I keep my health."

The old lady was attracted by the idea of making a bonus of fifty dollars, but she was cautious, and averse to parting with her money.

"I don't know what to say, Ferdinand," she replied. "Five hundred dollars is a good deal of money."

"So it is, aunt. Well, I don't know but I can offer you a little better terms. Give me four hundred and seventy-five, and I'll give you a note for five hundred and fifty. You can't make as much interest anywhere else."

"I'd like to accommodate you," said the old lady, hesitating, for, like most avaricious persons, she was captivated by the prospect of making extra-legal interest.

"I know you would. Aunt Deborah, but I don't want to ask the money as a favor. It is a strictly business transaction."

"I am afraid I couldn't spare more than four hundred and fifty."

"Very well, I won't dispute about the extra twenty-five dollars. Considering how much income I'm going to get, it isn't of any great importance."

"And you'll give me a note for five hundred and fifty?"

"Yes, certainly."

"I don't know as I ought to take so much interest."

"It's worth that to me, for though, of course, I could raise it by selling the ring, I don't like to do that."

"Well, I don't know but I'll do it. I'll get some ink, and you can write me the due bill."

"Why, Aunt Deborah, you haven't got the money here, have you?"

"Yes, I've got it in the house. A man paid up a mortgage last week, and I haven't yet invested the money. I meant to put it in the savings bank."

"You wouldn't get but six per cent there. Now the bonus I offer you will be equal to about twenty per cent."

"And you really feel able to pay so much?"

"Yes, aunt; as I told you, it will be worth more than that to me."

"Well, Ferdinand, we'll settle the matter now. I'll go and get the money, and you shall give me the note and the ring."

"Triumph!" said the young man to himself, when the old lady had left the room. "You're badly sold, Aunt Deborah, but it's a good job for me. I didn't think I would have so little trouble."

Within fifteen minutes the money was handed over, and Aunt Deborah took charge of the note and the valuable diamond ring.

"Be careful of the ring, Aunt Deborah," said Ferdinand. "Remember, I expect to redeem it again."

"I'll take good care of it, nephew, never fear!"

"If it were a little smaller, you could wear it, yourself."

"How would Deborah Kensington look with a diamond ring? The neighbors would think I was crazy. No: I'll keep it in a safe place, but I won't wear it."

"Now, Aunt Deborah, I must speak about other arrangements. Don't you think it would be well to start for San Francisco as soon as possible? You know I enter upon my duties as soon as I get there."

"Yes, Ferdinand, I think you ought to."

"I wish I could spare the time to spend a week with you, aunt; but business is business, and my motto is, business before pleasure."

"And very proper, too, Ferdinand," said the old lady, approvingly.

"So I think I had better leave Centreville tomorrow."

"May be you had. You must write and let me know when you get there, and how you like your place."

"So I will, and I shall be glad to know that you take an interest in me. Now, aunt, as I have some errands to do, I will walk to the village and come back about the middle of the afternoon."

"Won't you be back to dinner?"

"No, I think not, aunt."

"Very well, Ferdinand. Come as soon as you can."

Half an hour later, Ferdinand entered the office of the "Centreville Gazette."

"How do you do, Mr. Kensington?" said Clapp, eagerly. "Anything new?"

"I should like to speak with you a moment in private, Mr. Clapp."

"All right!"

Clapp put on his coat, and went outside, shutting the door behind him.

"Well," said Ferdinand, "I've succeeded."

"Have you got the money?"

"Yes, but not quite as much as I anticipated."

"Can't you carry out your plan?" asked Clapp, soberly, fearing he was to be left out in the cold.

"I've formed a new one. Instead of going to California, which is very expensive, we'll go out West, say to St. Louis, and try our fortune there. What do you say?"

"I'm agreed. Can Luke go too?"

"Yes. I'll take you both out there, and lend you fifty dollars each besides, and you shall pay me back as soon as you are able. Will you let your friend know?"

"Yes, I'll undertake that; but when do you propose to start?"

"To-morrow morning."

"Whew! That's short notice."

"I want to get away as soon as possible, for fear the old lady should change her mind, and want her money back."

"That's where you're right."

"Of course you must give up your situation at once, as there is short time to get ready."

"No trouble about that," said Clapp. "I've hated the business for a long time, and shall be only too glad to leave. It's the same with Luke. He won't shed many tears at leaving Centreville."

"Well, we'll all meet this evening at the hotel. I depend upon your both being ready to start in the morning."

"All right, I'll let Luke know."

It may be thought singular that Ferdinand should have made so liberal an offer to two comparative strangers; but, to do the young man justice, though he had plenty of faults, he was disposed to be generous when he had money, though he was not particular how he obtained it. Clapp and Luke Harrison he recognized as congenial spirits, and he was willing to sacrifice something to obtain their companionship. How long his fancy was likely to last was perhaps doubtful; but for the present he was eager to associate them with his own plans.

CHAPTER XXI.

HARRY IS PROMOTED.

Clapp re-entered the printing office highly elated.

"Mr. Anderson," said he to the editor, "I am going to leave you."

Ferguson and Harry Walton looked up in surprise, and Mr. Anderson asked,—

"Have you got another place?"

"No; I am going West."

"Indeed! How long have you had that in view?"

"Not long. I am going with Mr. Kensington."

"The one who just called on you?"

"Yes."

"How soon do you want to leave?"

"Now."

"That is rather short notice."

"I know it, but I leave town to-morrow morning."

"Well, I wish you success. Here is the money I owe you."

"Sha'n't we see you again, Clapp?" asked Ferguson.

"Yes; I'll just look in and say good-by. Now I must go home and get ready."

"Well, Ferguson," said Mr. Andersen, after Clapp's departure, "that is rather sudden."

"So I think."

"How can we get along with only two hands?"

"Very well, sir. I'm willing to work a little longer, and Harry here is a pretty quick compositor now. The fact is, there isn't enough work for three."

"Then you think I needn't hire another journeyman?"

"No."

"If you both work harder I must increase your wages, and then I shall save money."

"I sha'n't object to that," said Ferguson, smiling.

"Nor I," said Harry.

"I was intending at any rate to raise Harry's wages, as I find he does nearly as much as a journeyman. Hereafter I will give you five dollars a week besides your board."

"Oh, thank you, sir!" said Harry, overjoyed at his good fortune.

"As for you, Ferguson, if you will give me an hour more daily, I will add three dollars a week to your pay."

"Thank you, sir. I think I can afford now to give Mrs. Ferguson the new bonnet she was asking for this morning."

"I don't want to overwork you two, but if that arrangement proves satisfactory, we will continue it."

"I suppose you will be buying your wife a new bonnet too; eh, Harry?" said Ferguson.

"I may buy myself a new hat. Luke Harrison turned up his nose at my old one the other day."

"What will Luke do without Clapp? They were always together."

"Perhaps he is going too."

"I don't know where he will raise the money, nor Clapp either, for that matter."

"Perhaps their new friend furnishes the money."

"If he does, he is indeed a friend."

"Well, it has turned out to our advantage, at any rate, Harry.
Suppose you celebrate it by coming round and taking supper with me?"
"With the greatest pleasure."

Harry was indeed made happy by his promotion. Having been employed for some months on board-wages, he had been compelled to trench upon the small stock of money which he had saved up when in the employ of Prof. Henderson, and he had been unable to send any money to his father, whose circumstances were straitened, and who found it very hard to make both ends meet. That evening he wrote a letter to his father, in which he inclosed ten dollars remaining to him from his fund of savings, at the same time informing him of his promotion. A few days later, he received the following reply:—

"MY DEAR SON:

"Your letter has given me great satisfaction, for I conclude from your promotion that you have done your duty faithfully, and won the approbation of your employer. The wages you now earn will amply pay your expenses, while you may reasonably hope that they will be still further increased, as you become more skilful and experienced. I am glad to hear that you are using your leisure hours to such good purpose, and are trying daily to improve your education. In this way you may hope in time to qualify yourself for the position of an editor, which is an honorable and influential profession, to which I should be proud to have you belong.

"The money which you so considerately inclose comes at the right time. Your brother needs some new clothes, and this will enable me to provide them. We all send love, and hope to hear from you often.

"Your affectionate father,
"HIRAM WALTON."

Harry's promotion took place just before the beginning of September. During the next week the fall term of the Prescott Academy commenced, and the village streets again became lively with returning students. Harry was busy at the case, when Oscar Vincent entered the printing office, and greeted him warmly.

"How are you, Oscar?" said Harry, his face lighting up with pleasure. "I am glad to see you back. I would shake hands, but I am afraid you wouldn't like it," and Harry displayed his hands soiled with printer's ink.

"Well, we'll shake hands in spirit, then, Harry. How have you passed the time?"

"I have been very busy, Oscar."

"And I have been very lazy. I have scarcely opened a book, that is, a study-book, during the vacation. How much have you done in French?"

"I have nearly finished Telemachus."

"You have! Then you have done splendidly. By the way, Harry, I received the paper you sent, containing your essay. It does you credit, my boy."

Mr. Anderson, who was sitting at his desk, caught the last words.

"What is that, Harry?" he asked. "Have you been writing for the papers?"

Harry blushed.

"Yes, sir," he replied. "I have written two or three articles for the 'Boston Weekly Standard.'"

"Indeed! I should like to see them."

"You republished one of them in the 'Gazette,' Mr. Anderson," said Ferguson.
"What do you refer to?"

"Don't you remember an article on 'Ambition,' which you inserted some weeks ago?"

"Yes, it was a good article. Did you write it, Walton?"

"Yes, air."

"Why didn't you tell me of it?"

"He was too bashful," said Ferguson.

"I am glad to know that you can write," said the editor. "I shall call upon you for assistance, in getting up paragraphs occasionally."

"I shall be very glad to do what I can," said Harry, gratified.

"Harry is learning to be an editor," said Ferguson.

"I will give him a chance for practice, then," and Mr. Anderson returned to his exchanges.

"By the way, Oscar," said Harry, "I am not a printer's devil any longer. I am promoted to be a journeyman."

"I congratulate you, Harry, but what will Fitz do now? He used to take so much pleasure in speaking of you as a printer's devil."

"I am sorry to deprive him of that pleasure. Did you see much of him in vacation, Oscar?"

"I used to meet him almost every day walking down Washington Street, swinging a light cane, and wearing a stunning necktie, as usual."

"Is he coming back this term?"

"Yes, he came on the same train with me. Hasn't he called to pay his respects to you?"

"No," answered Harry, with a smile. "He hasn't done me that honor.
He probably expects me to make the first call."
"Well, Harry, I suppose you will be on hand next week, when the
Clionian holds its first meeting?"
"Yes, I will be there."

"And don't forget to call at my room before that time. I want to examine you in French, and see how much progress you have made."

"Thank you, Oscar."

"Now I must be going. I have got a tough Greek lesson to prepare for to-morrow. I suppose it will take me twice as long as usual. It is always hard to get to work again after a long vacation. So good-morning, and don't forget to call at my room soon—say to-morrow evening."

"I will come."

"What a gentlemanly fellow your friend is!" said Ferguson.

"What is his name, Harry?" asked Mr. Anderson.

"Oscar Vincent. His father is an editor in Boston."

"What! the son of John Vincent?" said Mr. Anderson, surprised.

"Yes, sir; do you know his father?"

"Only by reputation. He is a man of great ability."

"Oscar is a smart fellow, too, but not a hard student."

"I shall be glad to have you bring him round to the house some evening, Harry. I shall be glad to become better acquainted with him."

"Thank you, sir. I will give him the invitation."

It is very possible that Harry rose in the estimation of his employer, from his intimacy with the son of a man who stood so high in his own profession. At all events, Harry found himself from this time treated with greater respect and consideration than before, and Mr. Anderson often called upon him to write paragraphs upon local matters, so that his position might be regarded except as to pay, as that of an assistant editor.

CHAPTER XXII.

MISS DEBORAH'S EYES ARE OPENED.

Aunt Deborah felt that she had done a good stroke of business. She had lent Ferdinand four hundred and fifty dollars, and received in return a note for five hundred and fifty, secured by a diamond ring worth even more. She plumed herself on her shrewdness, though at times she felt a little twinge at the idea of the exorbitant interest which she had exacted from so near a relative.

"But he said the money was worth that to him," she said to herself in extenuation, "and he's goin' to get two thousand dollars a year. I didn't want to lend the money, I'd rather have had it in the savings bank, but I did it to obleege him."

By such casuistry Aunt Deborah quieted her conscience, and carefully put the ring away among her bonds and mortgages.

"Who'd think a little ring like that should be worth so much?" she said to herself. "It's clear waste of money. But then Ferdinand didn't buy it. It was give to him, and a very foolish gift it was too. Railly, it makes me nervous to have it to take care of. It's so little it might get lost easy."

Aunt Deborah plumed herself upon her shrewdness. It was not easy to get the advantage of her in a bargain, and yet she had accepted the ring as security for a considerable loan without once questioning its genuineness. She relied implicitly upon her nephew's assurance of its genuineness, just as she had relied upon his assertion of relationship. But the time was soon coming when she was to be undeceived.

One day, a neighbor stopped his horse in front of her house, and jumping out of his wagon, walked up to the door and knocked.

"Good-morning, Mr. Simpson," said the old lady, answering the knock herself; "won't you come in?"

"Thank you, Miss Deborah, I can't stop this morning. I was at the post-office just now, when I saw there was a letter for you, and thought I'd bring it along."

"A letter for me!" said Aunt Deborah in some surprise, for her correspondence was very limited. "Who's it from?"

"It is post-marked New York," said Mr. Simpson.

"I don't know no one in New York," said the old lady, fumbling in her pockets for her spectacles.

"Maybe it's one of your old beaux," said Mr. Simpson, humorously, a joke which brought a grim smile to the face of the old spinster. "But I must be goin'. If it's an offer of marriage, don't forget to invite me to the wedding."

Aunt Deborah went into the house, and seating herself in her accustomed place, carefully opened the letter. She turned over the page, and glanced at the signature. To her astonishment it was signed,

"Your affectionate nephew,
"FERDINAND B. KENSINGTON."

"Ferdinand!" she exclaimed in surprise. "Why, I thought he was in Californy by this time. How could he write from New York? I s'pose he'll explain. I hope he didn't lose the money I lent him."

The first sentence in the letter was destined to surprise Miss Deborah yet more.

"Dear aunt," it commenced, "it is so many years since we have met, that I am afraid you have forgotten me."

"So many years!" repeated Miss Deborah in bewilderment. "What on earth can Ferdinand mean? Why, it's only five weeks yesterday since he was here. He must be crazy."

She resumed reading.

"I have often had it in mind to make you a little visit, but I have been so engrossed by business that I have been unable to get away. I am a salesman for A. T. Stewart, whom you must have heard of, as he is the largest retail dealer in the city. I have been three years in his employ, and have been promoted by degrees, till I now receive quite a good salary, until—and that is the news I have to write you—I have felt justifed in getting married. My wedding is fixed for next week, Thursday. I should be very glad if you could attend, though I suppose you would consider it a long journey. But at any rate I can assure you that I should be delighted to see you present on the occasion, and so would Maria. If you can't come, write to me, at any rate, in memory of old times. It is just possible that during our bridal tour—we are to go to the White Mountains for a week—we shall call on you. Let me know if it will be convenient for you to receive us for a day.

"Your affectionate nephew,
"FERDINAND B. KENSINGTON."

Miss Deborah read this letter like one dazed. She had to read it a second time before she could comprehend its purport.

"Ferdinand going to be married! He never said a word about it when he was here. And he don't say a word about Californy. Then again he says he hasn't seen me for years. Merciful man! I see it now—the other fellow was an impostor!" exclaimed Miss Deborah, jumping, to her feet in excitement. "What did he want to deceive an old woman for?"

It flashed upon her at once. He came after money, and he had succeeded only too well. He had carried away four hundred and fifty dollars with him. True, he had left a note, and security. But another terrible suspicion had entered the old lady's mind; the ring might not be genuine.

"I must know at once," exclaimed the disturbed spinster. "I'll go over to Brandon, to the jeweller's, and inquire. If it's paste, then, Deborah Kensington, you're the biggest fool in Centreville."

Miss Deborah summoned Abner, her farm servant from the field, and ordered him instantly to harness the horse, as she wanted to go to Brandon.

"Do you want me to go with you?" asked Abner.

"To be sure, I can't drive so fur, and take care of the horse."

"It'll interrupt the work," objected Abner.

"Never mind about the work," said Deborah, impatiently. "I must go right off. It's on very important business."

"Wouldn't it be best to go after dinner?"

"No, we'll get some dinner over there, at the tavern."

"What's got into the old woman?" thought Abner. "It isn't like her to spend money at a tavern for dinner, when she might as well dine at home. Interruptin' the work, too! However, it's her business!"

Deborah was ready and waiting when the horse drove up the door. She got in, and they set out. Abner tried to open a conversation, but he found Miss Deborah strangely unsocial. She appeared to take no interest in the details of farm work of which he spoke.

"Something's on her mind, I guess," thought Abner; and, as we know, he was right.

In her hand Deborah clutched the ring, of whose genuineness she had come to entertain such painful doubts. It might be genuine, she tried to hope, even if it came from an impostor; but her hope was small. She felt a presentiment that it would prove as false as the man from whom she received it. As for the story of the manner in which he became possessed of it, doubtless that was as false as the rest.

"How blind I was!" groaned Deborah in secret. "I saw he didn't look like the family. What a goose I was to believe that story about his changin' the color of his hair! I was an old fool, and that's all about it."

"Drive to the jeweller's," said Miss Deborah, when they reached
Brandon.
In some surprise, Abner complied.

Deborah got out of the wagon hastily and entered the store.

"What can I do for you, Miss Kensington?" asked the jeweller, who recognized the old lady.

"I want to show you a ring," said Aunt Deborah, abruptly. "Tell me what it's worth."

She produced the ring which the false Ferdinand had intrusted to her.

The jeweller scanned it closely.

"It's a good imitation of a diamond ring," he said.

"Imitation!" gasped Deborah.

"Yes; you didn't think it was genuine?"

"What's it worth?"

"The value of the gold. That appears to be genuine. It may be worth three dollars."

"Three dollars!" ejaculated Deborah. "He told me it cost six hundred and fifty."

"Whoever told you that was trying to deceive you."

"You're sure about its being imitation, are you?"

"There can be no doubt about it."

"That's what I thought," muttered the old lady, her face pale and rigid. "Is there anything to pay?"

"Oh, no; I am glad to be of service to you."

"Good-afternoon, then," said Deborah, abruptly, and she left the store.

"Drive home, Abner, as quick as you can," she said.

"I haven't had any dinner," Abner remarked, "You said you'd get some at the tavern."

"Did I? Well, drive over there. I'm not hungry myself, but I'll pay for some dinner for you."

Poor Aunt Deborah! it was not the loss alone that troubled her, though she was fond of money; but it was humiliating to think that she had fallen such an easy prey to a designing adventurer. In her present bitter mood, she would gladly have ridden fifty miles to see the false Ferdinand hanged.

CHAPTER XXIII.

THE PLOT AGAINST FLETCHER.

The intimacy between Harry and Oscar Vincent continued, and, as during the former term, the latter volunteered to continue giving French lessons to our hero. These were now partly of a conversational character, and, as Harry was thoroughly in earnest, it was not long before he was able to speak quite creditably.

About the first of November, Fitzgerald Fletcher left the Prescott Academy, and returned to his home in Boston. It was not because he had finished his education, but because he felt that he was not appreciated by his fellow-students. He had been ambitious to be elected to an official position in the Clionian Society, but his aspirations were not gratified. He might have accepted this disappointment, and borne it as well as he could, had it not been aggravated by the elevation of Harry Walton to the presidency. To be only a common member, while a boy so far his social inferior was President, was more than Fitzgerald could stand. He was so incensed that upon the announcement of the vote he immediately rose to a point of order.

"Mr. President," he said warmly, "I must protest against this election. Walton is not a member of the Prescott Academy, and it is unconstitutional to elect him President."

"Will the gentleman point out the constitutional clause which has been violated by Walton's election?" said Oscar Vincent.

"Mr. President," said Fletcher, "this Society was founded by students of the Prescott Academy; and the offices should be confined to the members of the school."

Harry Walton rose and said: "Mr. President, my election has been a great surprise to myself. I had no idea that any one had thought of me for the position. I feel highly complimented by your kindness, and deeply grateful for it; but there is something in what Mr. Fletcher says. You have kindly allowed me to share in the benefits of the Society, and that satisfies me. I think it will be well for you to make another choice as President."

"I will put it to vote," said the presiding officer. "Those who are ready to accept Mr. Walton's resignation will signify it in the usual way."

Fletcher raised his hand, but he was alone.

"Those who are opposed," said the President.

Every other hand except Harry's was now raised.

"Mr. Walton, your resignation is not accepted," said the presiding officer. "I call upon you to assume the duties of your new position."

Harry rose, and, modestly advanced to the chair. "I have already thanked you, gentlemen," he said, "for the honor you have conferred upon me in selecting me as your presiding officer. I have only to add that I will discharge its duties to the best of my ability."

All applauded except Fletcher. He sat with an unpleasant scowl upon his face, and waited for the result of the balloting for Vice-President and Secretary. Had he been elected to either position, the Clionian would probably have retained his illustrious name upon its roll. But as these honors were conferred upon other members, he formed the heroic resolution no longer to remain a member.

"Mr. President," he said, when the last vote was announced, "I desire to terminate my connection with this Society."

"I hope Mr. Fletcher will reconsider his determination," said Harry from the chair.

"I would like to inquire the gentleman's reasons," said Tom Carver.

"I don't like the way in which the Society is managed," said Fletcher. "I predict that it will soon disband."

"I don't see any signs of it," said Oscar. "If the gentleman is really sincere, he should not desert the Clionian in the hour of danger."

"I insist upon my resignation," said Fletcher.

"I move that it be accepted," said Tom Carver.

"Second the motion," said the boy who sat next him.

The resignation was unanimously accepted. Fletcher ought to have felt gratified at the prompt granting of his request, but he was not. He had intended to strike dismay into the Society by his proposal to withdraw, but there was no consternation visible. Apparently they were willing to let him go.

He rose from his seat mortified and wrathful.

"Gentlemen," he said, "you have complied with my request, and I am deeply grateful. I no longer consider it an honor to belong to the Clionian. I trust your new President may succeed as well in his new office as he has in the capacity of a printer's devil."

Fletcher was unable to proceed, being interrupted by a storm of hisses, in the midst of which he hurriedly made his exit.

"He wanted to be President himself—that's what's the matter," said Tom Carver in a whisper to his neighbor. "But he couldn't blame us for not wanting to have him."

Other members of the Society came to the same conclusion, and it was generally said that Fletcher had done himself no good by his undignified resentment. His parting taunt levelled at Harry was regarded as mean and ungenerous, and only strengthened the sentiment in favor of our hero who bore his honors modestly. In fact Tom Carver, who was fond of fun, conceived a project for mortifying Fletcher, and readily obtained the co-operation of his classmates.

It must be premised that Fitz was vain of his reading and declamation. He had a secret suspicion that, if he should choose to devote his talents to the stage, he would make a second Booth. This self-conceit of his made it the more easy to play off the following joke upon him.

A fortnight later, the young ladies of the village proposed to hold a Fair to raise funds for some public object. At the head of the committee of arrangements was a sister of the doctor's wife, named Pauline Clinton. This will explain the following letter which, Fletcher received the succeeding day:—

"FITZGERALD FLETCHER, ESQ.—Dear Sir: Understanding that you are a superior reader, we should be glad of your assistance in lending eclat to the Fair which we propose to hold on the evening of the 29th. Will you be kind enough to occupy twenty minutes by reading such selections as in your opinion will be of popular interest? It is desirable that you should let me know as soon as possible what pieces you have selected, that they may be printed on the programme.

"Yours respectfully,
"PAULINE CLINTON,
"(for the Committee)."

This note reached Fletcher at a time when he was still smarting from his disappointment in obtaining promotion from the Clionian Society. He read it with a flushed and triumphant face. He never thought of questioning its genuineness. Was it not true that he was a superior reader? What more natural than that he should be invited to give eclat to the Fair by the exercise of his talents! He felt it to be a deserved compliment. It was a greater honor to be solicited to give a public reading than to be elected President of the Clionian Society.

"They won't laugh at me now," thought Fletcher.

He immediately started for Oscar's room to make known his new honors.

"How are you, Fitz?" said Oscar, who was in the secret, and guessed the errand on which he came.

"Very well, thank you, Oscar," answered Fletcher, in a stately manner.

"Anything new with you?" asked Oscar, carelessly.

"Not much," said Fletcher. "There's a note I just received.

"Whew!" exclaimed Oscar, in affected astonishment. "Are you going to accept?"

"I suppose I ought to oblige them," said Fletcher. "It won't be much trouble to me, you know."

"To be sure; it's in a good cause. But how did they hear of your reading?"

"Oh, there are no secrets in a small village like this," said Fletcher.

"It's certainly a great compliment. Has anybody else been invited to read?"

"I think not," said Fletcher, proudly. "They rely upon me."

"Couldn't you get a chance for me? It would be quite an honor, and I should like it for the sake of the family."

"I shouldn't feel at liberty to interfere with their arrangements," said Fletcher, who didn't wish to share the glory with any one. "Besides, you don't read well enough."

"Well, I suppose I must give it up," said Oscar, in a tone of resignation. "By the way, what have you decided to read?"

"I haven't quite made up my mind," said Fletcher, in a tone of importance. "I have only just received the invitation, you know."

"Haven't you answered it yet?"

"No; but I shall as soon as I go home. Good-night, Oscar."

"Good-night, Fitz."

"How mad Fitz will be when he finds he has been sold!" said Oscar to himself. "But he deserves it for treating Harry so meanly."

CHAPTER XXIV.

READING UNDER DIFFICULTIES.

On reaching home, Fletcher looked over his "Speaker," and selected three poems which he thought he could read with best effect. The selection made, he sat down to his desk, and wrote a reply to the invitation, as follows:—

"MISS PAULINE CLINTON: I hasten to acknowledge your polite invitation to occupy twenty minutes in reading choice selections at your approaching Fair. I have paid much attention to reading, and hope to be able to give pleasure to the large numbers who will doubtless honor the occasion with their presence. I have selected three poems,—Poe's Raven, the Battle of Ivry, by Macaulay, and Marco Bozarris, by Halleck. I shall be much pleased if my humble efforts add eclat to the occasion.

"Yours, very respectfully,
"FITZGERALD FLETCHER."

"There," said Fletcher, reading his letter through with satisfaction. "I think that will do. It is high-toned and dignified, and shows that I am highly cultured and refined. I will copy it off, and mail it."

Fletcher saw his letter deposited in the post-office, and returned to his room.

"I ought to practise reading these poems, so as to do it up handsomely," he said. "I suppose I shall get a good notice in the 'Gazette.' If I do, I will buy a dozen papers, and send to my friends. They will see that I am a person of consequence in Centreville, even if I didn't get elected to any office in the high and mighty Clionian Society."

I am sorry that I cannot reproduce the withering sarcasm which
Fletcher put into his tone in the last sentence.
When Demosthenes was practising oratory, he sought the sea-shore; but Fitzgerald repaired instead to a piece of woods about half a mile distant. It was rather an unfortunate selection, as will appear.

It so happened that Tom Carver and Hiram Huntley were strolling about the woods, when they espied Fletcher approaching with an open book in his hand.

"Hiram," said Tom, "there's fun coming. There's Fitz Fletcher with his 'Speaker' in his hand. He's going to practise reading in the woods. Let us hide, and hear the fun."

"I'm in for it," said Hiram, "but where will be the best place to hide?"

"Here in this hollow tree. He'll be very apt to halt here."

"All right! Go ahead, I'll follow."

They quickly concealed themselves in the tree, unobserved by
Fletcher, whose eyes were on his book.
About ten feet from the tree he paused.

"I guess this'll be a good place," he said aloud. "There's no one to disturb me here. Now, which shall I begin with? I think I'll try The Raven. But first it may be well to practise an appropriate little speech. Something like this:"—

Fletcher made a low bow to the assembled trees, cleared his throat, and commenced,—

"Ladies and Gentlemen: It gives me great pleasure to appear before you this evening, in compliance with the request of the committee, who have thought that my humble efforts would give eclat to the fair. I am not a professional reader, but I have ever found pleasure in reciting the noble productions of our best authors, and I hope to give you pleasure."

"That'll do, I think," said Fletcher, complacently. "Now I'll try
The Raven."
In a deep, sepulchral tone, Fletcher read the first verse, which is quoted below:—

"Once upon a midnight dreary, while I pondered weak and weary,
Over many a quaint and curious volume of forgotten lore,
While I nodded, nearly napping, suddenly there came a tapping,
As of some one gently rapping, rapping at my chamber door.
"Tis some visitor,' I muttered, 'tapping at my chamber door—
Only this and nothing more.'"

Was it fancy, or did Fletcher really hear a slow, measured tapping near him—upon one of the trees, as it seemed? He started, and looked nervously; but the noise stopped, and he decided that he had been deceived, since no one was visible.

The boys within the tree made no other demonstration till Fletcher had read the following verse:—

"Back into the chamber turning, all my soul within me burning,
Soon again I heard a tapping, something louder than before.
'Surely,' said I, 'surely that is something at my window lattice;
Let me see then what thereat is, and this mystery explore—
Let my heart be still a moment, and this mystery explore;
'Tis the wind, and nothing more.'"

Here an indescribable, unearthly noise was heard from the interior of the tree, like the wailing of some discontented ghost.

"Good heavens! what's that?" ejaculated Fletcher, turning pale, and looking nervously around him.

It was growing late, and the branches above him, partially stripped of their leaves, rustled in the wind. Fletcher was somewhat nervous, and the weird character of the poem probably increased this feeling, and made him very uncomfortable. He summoned up courage enough, however, to go on, though his voice shook a little. He was permitted to go on without interruption to the end. Those who are familiar with the poem, know that it becomes more and more wild and weird as it draws to the conclusion. This, with his gloomy surroundings, had its effect upon the mind of Fletcher. Scarcely had he uttered the last words, when a burst of wild and sepulchral laughter was heard within a few feet of him. A cry of fear proceeded from Fletcher, and, clutching his book, he ran at wild speed from the enchanted spot, not daring to look behind him. Indeed, he never stopped running till he passed out of the shadow of the woods, and was well on his way homeward.

Tom Carver and Hiram crept out from their place of concealment. They threw themselves on the ground, and roared with laughter.

"I never had such fun in my life," said Tom.

"Nor I."

"I wonder what Fitz thought."

"That the wood was enchanted, probably; he left in a hurry."

"Yes; he stood not on the order of his going, but went at once."

"I wish I could have seen him. We must have made a fearful noise."

"I was almost frightened myself. He must be almost home by this time."

"When do you think he'll find out about the trick?"

"About the invitation? Not till he gets a letter from Miss Clinton, telling him it is all a mistake. He will be terribly mortified."

Meanwhile Fletcher reached home, tired and out of breath. His temporary fear was over, but he was quite at sea as to the cause of the noises he had heard. He could not suspect any of his school-fellows, for no one was visible, nor had he any idea that any were in the wood at the time.

"I wonder if it was an animal," he reflected. "It was a fearful noise. I must find some other place to practise reading in. I wouldn't go to that wood again for fifty dollars."

But Fletcher's readings were not destined to be long continued. When he got home from school the next day, he found the following note, which had been left for him during the forenoon:—

"MR. FITZGERALD FLETCHER,—Dear Sir: I beg to thank you for your kind proposal to read at our Fair; but I think there must be some mistake in the matter, as we have never contemplated having any readings, nor have I written to you on the subject, as you intimate. I fear that we shall not have time to spare for such a feature, though, under other circumstances, it might be attractive. In behalf of the committee, I beg to tender thanks for your kind proposal.

"Yours respectfully,
"PAULINE CLINTON."

Fletcher read this letter with feelings which can better be imagined than described. He had already written home in the most boastful manner about the invitation he had received, and he knew that before he could contradict it, it would have been generally reported by his gratified parents to his city friends. And now he would be compelled to explain that he had been duped, besides enduring the jeers of those who had planned the trick.

This was more than he could endure. He formed a sudden resolution. He would feign illness, and go home the next day. He could let it be inferred that it was sickness alone which had compelled him to give up the idea of appearing as a public reader.

Fitz immediately acted upon his decision, and the next day found him on the way to Boston. He never returned to the Prescott Academy as a student.

CHAPTER XXV.

AN INVITATION TO BOSTON.

Harry was doubly glad that he was now in receipt of a moderate salary. He welcomed it as an evidence that he was rising in the estimation of his employer, which was of itself satisfactory, and also because in his circumstances the money was likely to be useful.

"Five dollars a week!" said Harry to himself. "Half of that ought to be enough to pay for my clothes and miscellaneous expenses, and the rest I will give to father. It will help him take care of the rest of the family."

Our hero at once made this proposal by letter. This is a paragraph from his father's letter in reply:—

"I am glad, my dear son, to find you so considerate and dutiful, as your offer indicates. I have indeed had a hard time in supporting my family, and have not always been able to give them the comforts I desired. Perhaps it is my own fault in part. I am afraid I have not the faculty of getting along and making money that many others have. But I have had an unexpected stroke of good fortune. Last evening a letter reached your mother, stating that her cousin Nancy had recently died at St. Albans, Vermont, and that, in accordance with her will, your mother is to receive a legacy of four thousand dollars. With your mother's consent, one-fourth of this is to be devoted to the purchase of the ten acres adjoining my little farm, and the balance will be so invested as to yield us an annual income of one hundred and eighty dollars. Many would think this a small addition to an income, but it will enable us to live much more comfortably. You remember the ten-acre lot to the east of us, belonging to the heirs of Reuben Todd. It is excellent land, well adapted for cultivation, and will fully double the value of my farm.

"You see, therefore, my dear son, that a new era of prosperity has opened for us. I am now relieved from the care and anxiety which for years have oppressed me, and feel sure of a comfortable support. Instead of accepting the half of your salary, I desire you, if possible, to save it, depositing in some reliable savings institution. If you do this every year till you are twenty-one, you will have a little capital to start you in business, and will be able to lead a more prosperous career than your father. Knowing you as well as I do, I do not feel it necessary to caution you against unnecessary expenditures. I will only remind you that extravagance is comparative, and that what would be only reasonable expenditure for one richer than yourself would be imprudent in you."

Harry read this letter with great joy. He was warmly attached to the little home circle, and the thought that they were comparatively provided for gave him fresh courage. He decided to adopt his father's suggestion, and the very next week deposited three dollars in the savings bank.

"That is to begin an account," he thought. "If I can only keep that up, I shall feel quite rich at the end of a year."

Several weeks rolled by, and Thanksgiving approached.

Harry was toiling at his case one day, when Oscar Vincent entered the office.

"Hard at work, I see, Harry," he said.

"Yes," said Harry; "I can't afford to be idle."

"I want you to be idle for three days," said Oscar.

Harry looked up in surprise.

"How is that?" he asked.

"You know we have a vacation from Wednesday to Monday at the Academy."

"Over Thanksgiving?"

"Yes."

"Well, I am going home to spend that time, and I want you to go with me."

"What, to Boston?" asked Harry, startled, for to him, inexperienced as he was, that seemed a very long journey.

"Yes. Father and mother gave me permission to invite you. Shall I show you the letter?"

"I'll take it for granted, Oscar, but I am afraid I can't go."

"Nonsense! What's to prevent?"

"In the first place, Mr. Anderson can't spare me."

"Ask him."

"What's that?" asked the editor, hearing his name mentioned.

"I have invited Harry to spend the Thanksgiving vacation with me in Boston, and he is afraid you can't spare him?"

"Does your father sanction your invitation?"

"Yes, he wrote me this morning—that is, I got the letter this morning—telling me to ask Harry to come."

Now the country editor had a great respect for the city editor, who was indeed known by reputation throughout New England as a man of influence and ability, and he felt disposed to accede to any request of his.

So he said pleasantly, "Of course, Harry, we shall miss you, but if Mr. Ferguson is disposed to do a little additional work, we will get along till Monday. What do you say, Mr. Ferguson?"

"I shall be very glad to oblige Harry," said the older workman, "and
I hope he will have a good time."
"That settles the question, Harry," said Oscar, joyfully. "So all you've got to do is to pack up and be ready to start to-morrow morning. It's Tuesday, you know, already."

Harry hesitated, and Oscar observed it.

"Well, what's the matter now?" he said; "out with it."

"I'll tell you, Oscar," said Harry, coloring a little. "Your father is a rich man, and lives handsomely. I haven't any clothes good enough to wear on a visit to your house."

"Oh, hang your clothes!" said Oscar, impetuously. "It isn't your clothes we invite. It's yourself."

"Still, Oscar—"

"Come, I see you think I am like Fitz Fletcher, after all. Say you think me a snob, and done with it."

"But I don't," said Harry, smiling.

"Then don't make any more ridiculous objections. Don't you think they are ridiculous, Mr. Ferguson?"

"They wouldn't be in some places," said Ferguson, "but here I think they are out of place. I feel sure you are right, and that you value Harry more than the clothes he wears."

"Well, Harry, do you surrender at discretion?" said Oscar. "You see
Ferguson is on my side."
"I suppose I shall have to," said Harry, "as long as you are not ashamed of me."

"None of that, Harry."

"I'll go."

"The first sensible words you've spoken this morning."

"I want to tell you how much I appreciate your kindness, Oscar," said
Harry, earnestly.
"Why shouldn't I be kind to my friend?"

"Even if he was once a printer's devil."

"Very true. It is a great objection, but still I will overlook it.
By the way, there is one inducement I didn't mention."
"What is that?"

"We may very likely see Fitz in the city. He is studying at home now, I hear. Who knows but he may get up a great party in your honor?"

"Do you think it likely?" asked Harry, smiling.

"It might not happen to occur to him, I admit. Still, if we made him a ceremonious call—"

"I am afraid he might send word that he was not at home."

"That would be a loss to him, no doubt. However, we will leave time to settle that question. Be sure to be on hand in time for the morning train."

"All right, Oscar."

Harry had all the love of new scenes natural to a boy of sixteen. He had heard so much of Boston that he felt a strong curiosity to see it. Besides, was not that the city where the "Weekly Standard" was printed, the paper in which he had already appeared as an author? In connection with this, I must here divulge a secret of Harry's. He was ambitious not only to contribute to the literary papers, but to be paid for his contributions. He judged that essays were not very marketable, and he had therefore in his leisure moments written a humorous sketch, entitled "The Tin Pedler's Daughter." I shall not give any idea of the plot here; I will only say that it was really humorous, and did not betray as much of the novice as might have been expected. Harry had copied it out in his best hand, and resolved to carry it to Boston, and offer it in person to the editor of the "Standard" with an effort, if accepted, to obtain compensation for it.

CHAPTER XXVI.

THE VINCENTS AT HOME.

When Harry rather bashfully imparted to Oscar his plans respecting the manuscript, the latter entered enthusiastically into them, and at once requested the privilege of reading the story. Harry awaited his judgment with some anxiety.

"Why, Harry, this is capital," said Oscar, looking up from the perusal.

"Do you really think so, Oscar?"

"If I didn't think so, I wouldn't say so."

"I thought you might say so out of friendship."

"I don't say it is the best I ever read, mind you, but I have read a good many that are worse. I think you managed the denouement (you're a French scholar, so I'll venture on the word) admirably."

"I only hope the editor of the 'Standard' will think so."

"If he doesn't, there are other papers in Boston; the 'Argus' for instance."

"I'll try the 'Standard' first, because I have already written for it."

"All right. Don't you want me to go to the office with you?"

"I wish you would. I shall be bashful."

"I am not troubled that way. Besides, my father's name is well known, and I'll take care to mention it. Sometimes influence goes farther than merit, you know."

"I should like to increase my income by writing for the city papers.
Even if I only made fifty dollars a year, it would all be clear gain."
Harry's desire was natural. He had no idea how many shared it. Every editor of a successful weekly could give information on this subject. Certainly there is no dearth of aspiring young writers—Scotts and Shakspeares in embryo—in our country, and if all that were written for publication succeeded in getting into print, the world would scarcely contain the books and papers which would pour in uncounted thousands from the groaning press.

When the two boys arrived in Boston they took a carriage to Oscar's house. It was situated on Beacon Street, not far from the Common,—a handsome brick house with a swell front, such as they used to build in Boston. No one of the family was in, and Oscar and Harry went up at once to the room of the former, which they were to share together. It was luxuriously furnished, so Harry thought, but then our hero had been always accustomed to the plainness of a country home.

"Now, old fellow, make yourself at home," said Oscar. "You can get yourself up for dinner. There's water and towels, and a brush."

"I don't expect to look very magnificent," said Harry. "You must tell your mother I am from the country."

"I would make you an offer if I dared," said Oscar.

"I am always open to a good offer."

"It's this: I'm one size larger than you, and my last year's suits are in that wardrobe. If any will fit you, they are yours."

"Thank you, Oscar," said Harry; "I'll accept your offer to-morrow."

"Why not to-day?"

"You may not understand me, but when I first appear before your family, I don't want to wear false colors."

"I understand," said Oscar, with instinctive delicacy.

An hour later, the bell rang for dinner.

Harry went down, and was introduced to his friend's mother and sister. The former was a true lady, refined and kindly, and her smile made our hero feel quite at home.

"I am glad to meet you, Mr. Walton," she said. "Oscar has spoken of you frequently."

With Oscar's sister Maud—a beautiful girl two years younger than himself—Harry felt a little more bashful; but the young lady soon entered into an animated conversation with him.

"Do you often come to Boston, Mr. Walton?" she asked.

"This is my first visit," said Harry.

"Then I dare say Oscar will play all sorts of tricks upon you. We had a cousin visit us from the country, and the poor fellow had a hard time."

"Yes," said Oscar, laughing, "I used to leave him at a street corner, and dodge into a doorway. It was amusing to see his perplexity when he looked about, and couldn't find me."

"Shall you try that on me?" asked Harry.

"Very likely."

"Then I'll be prepared."

"You might tie him with a rope, Mr. Walton," said Maud, "and keep firm hold."

"I will, if Oscar consents."

"I will see about it. But here is my father. Father, this is my friend, Harry Walton."

"I am glad to see you, Mr. Walton," said Mr. Vincent. "Then you belong to my profession?"

"I hope to, some time, sir; but I am only a printer as yet."

"You are yet to rise from the ranks. I know all about that. I was once a compositor."

Harry looked at the editor with great respect. He was stout, squarely built, with a massive head and a thoughtful expression. His appearance was up to Harry's anticipations. He felt that he would be prouder to be Mr. Vincent than any man in Boston, He could hardly believe that this man, who controlled so influential an organ, and was so honored in the community, was once a printer boy like himself.

"What paper are you connected with?" asked Mr. Vincent.

"The 'Centreville Gazette.'"

"I have seen it. It is quite a respectable paper."

"But how different," thought Harry, "from a great city daily!"

"Let us go out to dinner," said Mr. Vincent, consulting his watch.
"I have an engagement immediately afterward."
At table Harry sat between Maud and Oscar. If at first he felt a little bashful, the feeling soon wore away. The dinner hour passed very pleasantly. Mr. Vincent chatted very agreeably about men and things. There is no one better qualified to shine in this kind of conversation than the editor of a city daily, who is compelled to be exceptionally well informed. Harry listened with such interest that he almost forgot to eat, till Oscar charged him with want of appetite.

"I must leave in haste," said Mr. Vincent, when dinner was over.
"Oscar, I take it for granted that you will take care of your friend."
"Certainly, father. I shall look upon myself as his guardian, adviser and friend."

"You are not very well fitted to be a mentor, Oscar," said Maud.

"Why not, young lady?"

"You need a guardian yourself. You are young and frivolous."

"And you, I suppose, are old and judicious."

"Thank you. I will own to the last, and the first will come in time."

"Isn't it singular, Harry, that my sister should have so much conceit, whereas I am remarkably modest?"

"I never discovered it, Oscar," said Harry, smiling.

"That is right, Mr. Walton," said Maud. "I see you are on my side.
Look after my brother, Mr. Walton. He needs an experienced friend."
"I am afraid I don't answer the description, Miss Maud."

"I don't doubt you will prove competent. I wish you a pleasant walk."

"My sister's a jolly girl, don't you think so?" asked Oscar, as Maud left the room.

"That isn't exactly what I should say of her, but I can describe her as even more attractive than her brother."

"You couldn't pay her a higher compliment. But come; we'll take a walk on the Common."

They were soon on the Common, dear to every Bostonian, and sauntered along the walks, under the pleasant shade of the stately elms.

"Look there," said Oscar, suddenly; "isn't that Fitz Fletcher?"

"Yes," said Harry, "but he doesn't see us."

"We'll join him. How are you, Fitz?"

"Glad to see you, Oscar," said Fletcher, extending a gloved band, while in the other he tossed a light cane. "When did you arrive?"

"Only this morning; but you don't see Harry Walton."

Fletcher arched his brows in surprise, and said coldly, "Indeed, I was not aware Mr. Walton was in the city."

"He is visiting me," said Oscar.

Fletcher looked surprised. He knew the Vincents stood high socially, and it seemed extraordinary that they should receive a printer's devil as a guest.

"Have you given up the printing business?" he asked superciliously.

"No; I only have a little vacation from it."

"Ah, indeed! It's a very dirty business. I would as soon be a chimney-sweep."

"Each to his taste, Fitz," said Oscar. "If you have a taste for chimneys, I hope your father won't interfere."

"I haven't a taste for such a low business," said Fletcher, haughtily. "I should like it as well as being a printer's devil though."

"Would you? At any rate, if you take it up, you'll be sure to be well sooted."

Fletcher did not laugh at the joke. He never could see any wit in jokes directed at himself.

"How long are you going to stay at that beastly school?" he asked.

"I am not staying at any beastly school."

"I mean the Academy."

"Till I am ready for college. Where are you studying?"

"I recite to a private tutor."

"Well, we shall meet at 'Harvard' if we are lucky enough to get in."

Fletcher rather hoped Oscar would invite him to call at his house, for he liked to visit a family of high social position; but he waited in vain.

"What a fool Oscar makes of himself about that country clod-hopper!" thought the stylish young man, as he walked away. "The idea of associating with a printer's devil! I hope I know what is due to myself better."

CHAPTER XXVII.

THE OFFICE OF THE "STANDARD."

On the day after Thanksgiving, Harry brought out from his carpet-bag his manuscript story, and started with Oscar for the office of the "Weekly Standard." He bought the last copy of the paper, and thus ascertained the location of the office.

Oscar turned the last page, and ran through a sketch of about the same length as Harry's.

"Yours is fully as good as this, Harry," he said.

"The editor may not think so."

"Then he ought to."

"This story is by one of his regular contributors, Kenella Kent."

"You'll have to take a name yourself,—a nom de plume, I mean."

"I have written so far over the name of Franklin."

"That will do very well for essays, but is not appropriate for stories."

"Suppose you suggest a name, Oscar."

"How will 'Fitz Fletcher' do?"

"Mr. Fletcher would not permit me to take such a liberty."

"And you wouldn't want to take it."

"Not much."

"Let me see. I suppose I must task my invention, then. How will Old Nick do?"

"People would think you wrote the story."

"A fair hit. Hold on, I've got just the name. Frank Lynn."

"I thought you objected to that name."

"You don't understand me. I mean two names, not one. Frank Lynn! Don't you see?"

"Yes, it's a good plan. I'll adopt it."

"Who knows but you may make the name illustrious, Harry?"

"If I do, I'll dedicate my first boot to Oscar Vincent."

"Shake hands on that. I accept the dedication with mingled feelings of gratitude and pleasure."

"Better wait till you get it," said Harry, laughing. "Don't count your chickens before they're hatched."

"The first egg is laid, and that's something. But here we are at the office."

It was a building containing a large number of offices. The names of the respective occupants were printed on slips of black tin at the entrance. From this, Harry found that the office of the "Weekly Standard" was located at No. 6.

"My heart begins to beat, Oscar," said Harry, naturally excited in anticipation of an interview with one who could open the gates of authorship to him.

"Does it?" asked Oscar. "Mine has been beating for a number of years."

"You are too matter-of-fact for me, Oscar. If it was your own story, you might feel differently."

"Shall I pass it off as my own, and make the negotiation?"

Harry was half tempted to say yes, but it occurred to him that this might prove an embarrassment in the future, and he declined the proposal.

They climbed rather a dark, and not very elegant staircase, and found themselves before No. 6.

Harry knocked, or was about to do so, when a young lady with long ringlets, and a roll of manuscript in her hand, who had followed them upstairs advanced confidently, and, opening the door, went in. The two boys followed, thinking the ceremony of knocking needless.

They found themselves in a large room, one corner of which was partitioned off for the editor's sanctum. A middle-aged man was directing papers in the larger room, while piles of papers were ranged on shelves at the sides of the apartment.

The two boys hesitated to advance, but the young lady in ringlets went on, and entered the office through the open door.

"We'll wait till she is through," said Harry.

It was easy to hear the conversation that passed between the young lady and the editor, whom they could not see.

"Good-morning, Mr. Houghton," she said.

"Good-morning. Take a seat, please," said the editor, pleasantly.
"Are you one of our contributors?"
"No, sir, not yet," answered the young lady, "but I would become so."

"We are not engaging any new contributors at present, but still if you have brought anything for examination you may leave it."

"I am not wholly unknown to fame," said the young lady, with an air of consequence. "You have probably heard of Prunella Prune."

"Possibly, but I don't at present recall it. We editors meet with so many names, you know. What is the character of your articles?"

"I am a poetess, sir, and I also write stories."

"Poetry is a drug in the market. We have twice as much offered us as we can accept. Still we are always glad to welcome really meritorious poems."

"I trust my humble efforts will please you," said Prunella. "I have here some lines to a nightingale, which have been very much praised in our village. Shall I read them?"

"If you wish," said the editor, by no means cheerfully.

Miss Prune raised her voice, and commenced:—

"O star-eyed Nightingale,
How nobly thou dost sail
Through the air!
No other bird can compare
With the tuneful song
Which to thee doth belong.
I sit and hear thee sing,
While with tireless wing
  Thou dost fly.
And it makes me feel so sad,
It makes me feel so bad,
  I know not why,
And I heave so many sighs,
O warbler of the skies!"

"Is there much more?" asked the editor.

"That is the first verse. There are fifteen more," said Prunella.

"Then I think I shall not have time at present to hear you read it all. You may leave it, and I will look it over at my leisure."

"If it suits you," said Prunella, "how much will it be worth?"

"I don't understand."

"How much would you be willing to pay for it?"

"Oh, we never pay for poems," said Mr. Houghton.

"Why not?" asked Miss Prune, evidently disappointed.

"Our contributors are kind enough to send them gratuitously."

"Is that fostering American talent?" demanded Prunella, indignantly.

"American poetical talent doesn't require fostering, judging from the loads of poems which are sent in to us."

"You pay for stories, I presume?"

"Yes, we pay for good, popular stories."

"I have one here," said Prunella, untying her manuscript, "which I should like to read to you."

"You may read the first paragraph, if you please. I haven't time to hear more. What is the title?"

"'The Bandit's Bride.' This is the way it opens:—

"'The night was tempestuous. Lightnings flashed in the cerulean sky, and the deep-voiced thunder rolled from one end of the firmament to the other. It was a landscape in Spain. From a rocky defile gayly pranced forth a masked cavalier, Roderigo di Lima, a famous bandit chief.

"'"Ha! ha!" he laughed in demoniac glee, "the night is well fitted to my purpose. Ere it passes, Isabella Gomez shall be mine."'"

"I think that will do," said Mr. Houghton, hastily. "I am afraid that style won't suit our readers."

"Why not?" demanded Prunella, sharply. "I can assure you, sir, that it has been praised by excellent judges in our village."

"It is too exciting for our readers. You had better carry it to 'The
Weekly Corsair.'"
"Do they pay well for contributions?"

"I really can't say. How much do you expect?"

"This story will make about five columns. I think twenty-five dollars will be about right."

"I am afraid you will be disappointed. We can't afford to pay such prices, and the 'Corsair' has a smaller circulation than our paper."

"How much do you pay?"

"Two dollars a column."

"I expected more," said Prunella, "but I will write for you at that price."

"Send us something suited to our paper, and we will pay for it at that price."

"I will write you a story to-morrow. Good-morning, sir."

"Good-morning, Miss Prune."

The young lady with ringlets sailed out of the editor's room, and Oscar, nudging Harry, said, "Now it is our turn. Come along. Follow me, and don't be frightened."

CHAPTER XXVIII.

ACCEPTED.

The editor of the "Standard" looked with some surprise at the two boys. As editor, he was not accustomed to receive such young visitors. He was courteous, however, and said, pleasantly:—

"What can I do for you, young gentlemen?"

"Are you the editor of the 'Standard'?" asked Harry, diffidently.

"I am. Do you wish to subscribe?"

"I have already written something for your paper," Harry continued.

"Indeed!" said the editor. "Was it poetry or prose?"

Harry felt flattered by the question. To be mistaken for a poet he felt to be very complimentary. If he had known how much trash weekly found its way to the "Standard" office, under the guise of poetry, he would have felt less flattered.

"I have written some essays over the name of 'Franklin,'" he hastened to say.

"Ah, yes, I remember, and very sensible essays too. You are young to write."

"Yes, sir; I hope to improve as I grow older."

By this time Oscar felt impelled to speak for his friend. It seemed to him that Harry was too modest.

"My friend is assistant editor of a New Hampshire paper,—'The Centreville Gazette,'" he announced.
"Indeed!" said the editor, looking surprised. "He is certainly young for an editor."

"My friend is not quite right," said Harry, hastily. "I am one of the compositors on that paper."

"But you write editorial paragraphs," said Oscar.

"Yes, unimportant ones."

"And are you, too, an editor?" asked the editor of the "Standard," addressing Oscar with a smile.

"Not exactly," said Oscar; "but I am an editor's son. Perhaps you are acquainted with my father,—John Vincent of this city."

"Are you his son?" said the editor, respectfully. "I know your father slightly. He is one of our ablest journalists."

"Thank you, sir."

"I am very glad to receive a visit from you, and should be glad to print anything from your pen."

"I am not sure about that," said Oscar, smiling. "If I have a talent for writing, it hasn't developed itself yet. But my friend here takes to it as naturally as a duck takes to water."

"Have you brought me another essay, Mr. 'Franklin'?" asked the editor, turning to Harry. "I address you by your nom de plume, not knowing your real name."

"Permit me to introduce my friend, Harry Walton," said Oscar.
"Harry, where is your story?"
"I have brought you in a story," said Harry, blushing. "It is my first attempt, and may not suit you, but I shall be glad if you will take the trouble to examine it."

"With pleasure," said the editor. "Is it long?"

"About two columns. It is of a humorous character."

The editor reached out his hand, and, taking the manuscript, unrolled it. He read the first few lines, and they seemed to strike his attention.

"If you will amuse yourselves for a few minutes, I will read it at once," he said. "I don't often do it, but I will break over my custom this time."

"Thank you, sir," said Harry.

"There are some of my exchanges," said the editor, pointing to a pile on the floor. "You may find something to interest you in some of them."

They picked up some papers, and began to read. But Harry could not help thinking of the verdict that was to be pronounced on his manuscript. Upon that a great deal hinged. If he could feel that he was able to produce anything that would command compensation, however small, it would make him proud and happy. He tried, as he gazed furtively over his paper at the editor's face, to anticipate his decision, but the latter was too much accustomed to reading manuscript to show the impression made upon him.

Fifteen minutes passed, and he looked up.

"Well, Mr. Walton," he said, "your first attempt is a success."

Harry's face brightened.

"May I ask if the plot is original?"

"It is so far as I know, sir. I don't think I ever read anything like it."

"Of course there are some faults in the construction, and the dialogue might be amended here and there. But it is very creditable, and I will use it in the 'Standard' if you desire it."

"I do, sir."

"And how much are you willing to pay for it?" Oscar struck in.

The editor hesitated.

"It is not our custom to pay novices just at first," he said. "If Mr. Walton keeps on writing, he would soon command compensation."
Harry would not have dared to press the matter, but Oscar was not so diffident. Indeed, it is easier to be bold in a friend's cause than one's own.

"Don't you think it is worth being paid for, if it is worth printing?" he persisted.

"Upon that principle, we should feel obliged to pay for poetry," said the editor.

"Oh," said Oscar, "poets don't need money. They live on flowers and dew-drops."

The editor smiled.

"You think prose-writers require something more substantial?"

"Yes, sir."

"I will tell you how the matter stands," said the editor. "Mr. Walton is a beginner. He has his reputation to make. When it is made he will be worth a fair price to me, or any of my brother editors."

"I see," said Oscar; "but his story must be worth something. It will fill up two columns. If you didn't print it, you would have to pay somebody for writing these two columns."

"You have some reason in what you say. Still our ordinary rule is based on justice. A distinction should be made between new contributors and old favorites."

"Yes, sir. Pay the first smaller sums."

If the speaker had not been John Vincent's son, it would have been doubtful if his reasoning would have prevailed. As it was, the editor yielded.

"I may break over my rule in the case of your friend," said the editor; "but he must be satisfied with a very small sum for the present."

"Anything will satisfy me, sir," said Harry, eagerly.

"Your story will fill two columns. I commonly pay two dollars a column for such articles, if by practised writers. I will give you half that."

"Thank you, sir. I accept it," said Harry, promptly.

"In a year or so I may see my way clear to paying you more, Mr. Walton; but you must consider that I give you the opportunity of winning popularity, and regard this as part of your compensation, at present."

"I am quite satisfied, sir," said Harry, his heart fluttering with joy and triumph. "May I write you some more sketches?"

"I shall be happy to receive and examine them; but you must not be disappointed if from time to time I reject your manuscripts."

"No, sir; I will take it as a hint that they need improving."

"I will revise my friend's stories, sir," said Oscar, humorously, "and give him such hints as my knowledge of the world may suggest."

"No doubt such suggestions from so mature a friend will materially benefit them," said the editor, smiling.

He opened his pocket-book, and, drawing out a two-dollar bill, handed it to Harry.

"I shall hope to pay you often," he said, "for similar contributions."

"Thank you, sir," said Harry.

Feeling that their business was at an end, the boys withdrew. As they reached the foot of the stairs, Oscar took off his cap, and bowed low.

"Mr. Lynn, I congratulate you," he said.

"I can't tell you how glad I feel, Oscar," said Harry, his face radiant.

"Let me suggest that you owe me a commission for impressing upon the editor the propriety of paying you."

"How much do you ask?"

"An ice-cream will be satisfactory."

"All right."

"Come round to Copeland's then. We'll celebrate your success in a becoming manner."

CHAPTER XXIX.

MRS. CLINTON'S PARTY.

When Oscar and Harry reached home they were met by Maud, who flourished in her hand what appeared to be a note.

"What is it, Maud?" asked Oscar. "A love-letter for me?"

"Don't flatter yourself, Oscar. No girl would be so foolish as to write you a love-letter. It is an invitation to a party on Saturday evening."

"Where?"

"At Mrs. Clinton's."

"I think I will decline," said Oscar. "I wouldn't like to leave Harry alone."
"Oh, he is included too. Mrs. Clinton heard of his being here, and expressly included him in the invitation."

"That alters the case. You'll go, Harry, won't you?"

"I am afraid I shouldn't know how to behave at a fashionable party," said Harry.

"Oh, you've only got to make me your model," said Oscar, "and you'll be all right."

"Did you ever see such conceit, Mr. Walton?" said Maud.

"It reminds me of Fletcher," said Harry.

"Fitz Fletcher? By the way, he will probably be there. His family are acquainted with the Clintons."

"Yes, he is invited," said Maud.

"Good! Then there's promise of fun," said Oscar. "You'll see Fitz with his best company manners on."

"I am afraid he won't enjoy meeting me there," said Harry.

"Probably not."

"I don't see why," said Maud.

"Shall I tell, Harry?"

"Certainly."

"To begin with, Fletcher regards himself as infinitely superior to Walton here, because his father is rich, and Walton's poor. Again, Harry is a printer, and works for a living, which Fitz considers degrading. Besides all this, Harry was elected President of our Debating Society,—an office which Fitz wanted."
"I hope" said Maud, "that Mr. Fletcher's dislike does not affect your peace of mind, Mr. Walton."

"Not materially," said Harry, laughing.

"By the way, Maud," said Oscar, "did I ever tell you how Fletcher's pride was mortified at school by our discovering his relationship to a tin-pedler?"

"No, tell me about it."

The story, already familiar to the reader, was graphically told by
Oscar, and served to amuse his sister.
"He deserved the mortification," she said. "I shall remember it if he shows any of his arrogance at the party."

"Fletcher rather admires Maud," said Oscar, after his sister had gone out of the room; "but the favor isn't reciprocated. If he undertakes to say anything to her against you, she will take him down, depend upon it."

Saturday evening came, and Harry, with Oscar and his sister, started for the party. Our hero, having confessed his inability to dance, had been diligently instructed in the Lancers by Oscar, so that he felt some confidence in being able to get through without any serious blunder.

"Of course you must dance, Harry," he said. "You don't want to be a wall-flower."

"I may have to be," said Harry. "I shall know none of the young ladies except your sister."

"Maud will dance the first Lancers with you, and I will get you a partner for the second."

"You may dispose of me as you like, Oscar."

"Wisely said. Don't forget that I am your Mentor."

When they entered the brilliantly lighted parlors, they were already half full. Oscar introduced his friend to Mrs. Clinton.

"I am glad to see you here, Mr. Walton," said the hostess, graciously. "Oscar, I depend upon you to introduce your friend to some of the young ladies."

"You forget my diffidence, Mrs. Clinton."

"I didn't know you were troubled in that way.'"

"See how I am misjudged. I am painfully bashful."

"You hide it well," said the hostess, with a smile.

"Escort my sister to a seat, Harry," said Oscar. "By the way, you two will dance in the first Lancers."

"If Miss Maud will accept so awkward a partner," said Harry.

"Oh, yes, Mr. Walton. I'll give you a hint if you are going wrong."

Five minutes later Fletcher touched Oscar on the shoulder.

"Oscar, where is your sister?" he asked.

"There," said Oscar, pointing her out.

Fletcher, who was rather near-sighted, did not at first notice that Harry Walton was sitting beside the young lady. He advanced, and made a magnificent bow, on which he rather prided himself.

"Good-evening, Miss Vincent," he said.

"Good-evening, Mr. Fletcher."

"I am very glad you have favored the party with your presence."

"Thank you, Mr. Fletcher. Don't turn my head with your compliments."

"May I hope you will favor me with your hand in the first Lancers?"

"I am sorry, Mr. Fletcher, but I am engaged to Mr. Walton. I believe you are acquainted with him."

Fletcher for the first time observed our hero, and his face wore a look of mingled annoyance and scorn.

"I have met the gentleman," he said, haughtily.

"Mr. Fletcher and I have met frequently," said Harry, pleasantly.

"I didn't expect to meet you here," said Fletcher with marked emphasis.

"Probably not," said Harry. "My invitation is due to my being a friend of Oscar's."

"I was not aware that you danced," said Fletcher who was rather curious on the subject.

"I don't—much."

"Where did you learn—in the printing office?"

"No, in the city."

"Ah! Indeed!"

Fletcher thought he had wasted time enough on our hero, and turned again to Maud.

"May I have the pleasure of your hand in the second dance?" he asked.

"I will put you down for that, if you desire it."

"Thank you."

It so happened that when Harry and Maud took the floor, they found Fletcher their vis-a-vis. Perhaps it was this that made Harry more emulous to get through without making any blunders. At any rate, he succeeded, and no one in the set suspected that it was his first appearance in public as a dancer.

Fletcher was puzzled. He had hoped that Harry would make himself ridiculous, and throw the set into confusion. But the dance passed off smoothly, and in due time Fletcher led out Maud. If he had known his own interest, he would have kept silent about Harry, but he had little discretion.

"I was rather surprised to see Walton here," he began.

"Didn't you know he was in the city?

"Yes, I met him with Oscar."

"Then why were you surprised?"

"Because his social position does not entitle him to appear in such a company. When I first knew him, he was only a printer's apprentice."

Fletcher wanted to say printer's devil, but did not venture to do so in presence of a young lady.

"He will rise higher than that."

"I dare say," said Fletcher, with a sneer, "he will rise in time to be a journeyman with a salary of fifteen dollars a week."

"If I am not mistaken in Mr. Walton, he will rise much higher than that. Many of our prominent men have sprung from beginnings like his."

"It must be rather a trial to him to come here. His father is a day-laborer, I believe, and of course he has never been accustomed to any refinement or polish."

"I don't detect the absence of either," said Maud, quietly.

"Do you believe in throwing down all social distinctions, and meeting the sons of laborers on equal terms?"

"As to that," said Maud, meeting her partner's glance, "I am rather democratic. I could even meet the son of a tin-pedler on equal terms, provided he were a gentleman."

The blood rushed to Fletcher's cheeks.

"A tin-pedler!" he ejaculated.

"Yes! Suppose you were the son, or relation, of a tin-pedler, why should I consider that? It would make you neither better nor worse."

"I have no connection with tin-pedlers," said Fletcher, hastily.
"Who told you I had?"

"I only made a supposition, Mr. Fletcher."

But Fletcher thought otherwise. He was sure that Maud had heard of his mortification at school, and it disturbed him not a little, for, in spite of her assurance, he felt that she believed the story, and it annoyed him so much that he did not venture to make any other reference to Harry.

"Poor Fitz!" said Oscar, when on their way home Maud gave an account of their conversation, "I am afraid he will murder the tin-pedler some time, to get rid of such an odious relationship."

CHAPTER XXX.

TWO LETTERS FROM THE WEST.

The vacation was over all too soon, yet, brief as it was, Harry looked back upon it with great satisfaction. He had been kindly received in the family of a man who stood high in the profession which he was ambitious to enter; he had gratified his curiosity to see the chief city of New England; and, by no means least, he had secured a position as paid contributor for the "Standard."

"I suppose you will be writing another story soon," said Oscar.

"Yes," said Harry, "I have got the plan of one already."

"If you should write more than you can get into the 'Standard,' you had better send something to the 'Weekly Argus.'"

"I will; but I will wait till the 'Standard' prints my first sketch, so that I can refer to that in writing to the 'Argus.'"

"Perhaps you are right. There's one advantage to not presenting yourself. They won't know you're only a boy."

"Unless they judge so from my style."

"I don't think they would infer it from that. By the way, Harry, suppose my father could find an opening for you as a reporter on his paper,—would you be willing to accept it?"

"I am not sure whether it would be best for me," said Harry, slowly, "even if I were qualified."

"There is more chance to rise on a city paper."

"I don't know. If I stay here I may before many years control a paper of my own. Then, if I want to go into politics, there would be more chance in the country than in the city."

"Would you like to go into politics?"

"I am rather too young to decide about that; but if I could be of service in that way, I don't see why I should not desire it."

"Well, Harry, I think you are going the right way to work."

"I hope so. I don't want to be promoted till I am fit for it. I am going to work hard for the next two or three years."

"I wish I were as industrious as you are, Harry."

"And I wish I knew as much as you do, Oscar."

"Say no more, or we shall be forming a Mutual Admiration Society," said Oscar, laughing.

Harry received a cordial welcome back to the printing office. Mr. Anderson asked him many questions about Mr. Vincent; and our hero felt that his employer regarded him with increased consideration, on account of his acquaintance with the great city editor. This consideration was still farther increased when Mr. Anderson learned our hero's engagement by the "Weekly Standard."

Three weeks later, the "Standard" published Harry's sketch, and accepted another, at the same price. Before this latter was printed, Harry wrote a third sketch, which he called "Phineas Popkin's Engagement." This he inclosed to the "Weekly Argus," with a letter in which he referred to his engagement by the "Standard." In reply he received the following letter:—

"BOSTON, Jan., 18—,

"MR. FRANK LYNN,—Dear Sir: We enclose three dollars for your sketch,—'Phineas Popkin's Engagement.' We shall be glad to receive other sketches, of similar character and length, and, if accepted, we will pay the same price therefor.

"I. B. FITCH & Co."

This was highly satisfactory to Harry. He was now an accepted contributor to two weekly papers, and the addition to his income would be likely to reach a hundred dollars a year. All this he would be able to lay up, and as much or more from his salary on the "Gazette." He felt on the high road to success. Seeing that his young compositor was meeting with success and appreciation abroad, Mr. Anderson called upon him more frequently to write paragraphs for the "Gazette." Though this work was gratuitous, Harry willingly undertook it. He felt that in this way he was preparing himself for the career to which he steadily looked forward. Present compensation, he justly reasoned, was of small importance, compared with the chance of improvement. In this view, Ferguson, who proved to be a very judicious friend, fully concurred. Indeed Harry and he became more intimate than before, if that were possible, and they felt that Clapp's departure was by no means to be regretted. They were remarking this one day, when Mr. Anderson, who had been examining his mail, looked up suddenly, and said, "What do you think, Mr. Ferguson? I've got a letter from Clapp."

"A letter from Clapp? Where is he?" inquired Ferguson, with interest.

"This letter is dated at St. Louis. He doesn't appear to be doing very well."

"I thought he was going to California."

"So he represented. But here is the letter." Ferguson took it, and, after reading, handed it to Harry.

It ran thus:—

"ST. LOUIS, April 4, 18—.

"JOTHAM ANDERSON, ESQ.,—Dear Sir: Perhaps you will be surprised to hear from me, but I feel as if I would like to hear from Centreville, where I worked so long. The man that induced me and Harrison to come out here left us in the lurch three days after we reached St. Louis. He said he was going on to San Francisco, and he had only money enough to pay his own expenses. As Luke and I were not provided with money, we had a pretty hard time at first, and had to pawn some of our clothes, or we should have starved. Finally I got a job in the 'Democrat' office, and a week after, Luke got something to do, though it didn't pay very well. So we scratched along as well as we could. Part of the time since we have been out of work, and we haven't found 'coming West' all that it was cracked up to be.

"Are Ferguson and Harry Walton still working for you? I should like to come back to the 'Gazette' office, and take my old place; but I haven't got five dollars ahead to pay my travelling expenses. If you will send me out thirty dollars, I will come right on, and work it out after I come back. Hoping for an early reply, I am,

"Yours respectfully,
"HENRY CLAPP."

"Are you going to send out the money, Mr. Anderson?" asked Ferguson.

"Not I. Now that Walton has got well learnt, I don't need another workman. I shall respectfully decline his offer."

Both Harry and Ferguson were glad to hear this, for they felt that Clapp's presence would be far from making the office more agreeable.

"Here's a letter for you, Walton, also post-marked St. Louis," said Mr. Anderson, just afterward.

Harry took it with surprise, and opened it at once.

"It's from Luke Harrison," he said, looking at the signature.

"Does he want you to send him thirty dollars?" asked Ferguson.

"Listen and I will read the letter."

"DEAR HARRY," it commenced, "you will perhaps think it strange that I have written to you; but we used to be good friends. I write to tell you that I don't like this place. I haven't got along well, and I want to get back. Now I am going to ask of you a favor. Will you lend me thirty or forty dollars, to pay my fare home? I will pay you back in a month or two months sure, after I get to work. I will also pay you the few dollars which I borrowed some time ago. I ought to have done it before, but I was thoughtless, and I kept putting it off. Now, Harry, I know you have the money, and you can lend it to me just as well as not, and

I'll be sure to pay it back before you need it. Just get a post-office order, and send it to Luke Harrison, 17 R—— Street, St. Louis, and I'll be sure to get it. Give my respects to Mr. Anderson, and also to Mr. Ferguson.

"Your friend,
"LUKE HARRISON."
"There is a chance for a first-class investment, Harry," said
Ferguson.
"Do you want to join me in it?"

"No, I would rather pay the money to have 'your friend' keep away."

"I don't want to be unkind or disobliging," said Harry, "but I don't feel like giving Luke this money. I know he would never pay me back."

"Say no, then."

"I will. Luke will be mad, but I can't help it."

So both Mr. Anderson and Harry wrote declining to lend. The latter, in return, received a letter from Luke, denouncing him as a "mean, miserly hunks;" but even this did not cause him to regret his decision.

CHAPTER XXXI.

ONE STEP UPWARD.

In real life the incidents that call for notice do not occur daily. Months and years pass, sometimes, where the course of life is quiet and uneventful. So it was with Harry Walton. He went to his daily work with unfailing regularity, devoted a large part of his leisure to reading and study, or writing sketches for the Boston papers, and found himself growing steadily wiser and better informed. His account in the savings-bank grew slowly, but steadily; and on his nineteenth birthday, when we propose to look in upon him again, he was worth five hundred dollars.

Some of my readers who are favored by fortune may regard this as a small sum. It is small in itself, but it was not small for a youth in Harry's position to have saved from his small earnings. But of greater value than the sum itself was the habit of self-denial and saving which our hero had formed. He had started in the right way, and made a beginning which was likely to lead to prosperity in the end. It had not been altogether easy to save this sum. Harry's income had always been small, and he might, without incurring the charge of excessive extravagance, have spent the whole. He had denied himself on many occasions, where most boys of his age would have yielded to the temptation of spending money for pleasure or personal gratification; but he had been rewarded by the thought that he was getting on in the world.

"This is my birthday, Mr. Ferguson," he said, as he entered the printing-office on that particular morning.

"Is it?" asked Ferguson, looking up from his case with interest.
"How venerable are you, may I ask?"
"I don't feel very venerable as yet," said Harry, with a smile. "I am nineteen."

"You were sixteen when you entered the office."

"As printer's devil—yes."

"You have learned the business pretty thoroughly. You are as good a workman as I now, though I am fifteen years older."

"You are too modest, Mr. Ferguson."

"No, it is quite true. You are as rapid and accurate as I am, and you ought to receive as high pay."

"That will come in time. You know I make something by writing for the papers."

"That's extra work. How much did you make in that way last year?"

"I can tell you, because I figured it up last night. It was one hundred and twenty-five dollars, and I put every cent into the savings-bank."

"That is quite an addition to your income."

"I shall make more this year. I am to receive two dollars a column, hereafter, for my sketches."

"I congratulate you, Harry,—the more heartily, because I think you deserve it. Your recent sketches show quite an improvement over those you wrote a year ago."

"Do you really think so?" said Harry, with evident pleasure.

"I have no hesitation in saying so. You write with greater ease than formerly, and your style is less that of a novice."

"So I have hoped and thought; but of course I was prejudiced in my own favor."

"You may rely upon it. Indeed, your increased pay is proof of it.
Did you ask it?"
"The increase? No, the editor of the 'Standard' wrote me voluntarily that he considered my contributions worth the additional amount."

"That must be very pleasant. I tell you what, Harry, I've a great mind to set up opposition to you in the story line."

"Do so," said Harry, smiling.

"I would if I had the slightest particle of imagination; but the fact is, I'm too practical and matter-of-fact. Besides, I never had any talent for writing of any kind. Some time I may become publisher of a village paper like this; but farther than that I don't aspire."

"We are to be partners in that, you know, Ferguson."

"That may be, for a time; but you will rise higher than that, Harry."

"I am afraid you overrate me."

"No; I have observed you closely in the time we have been together, and I have long felt that you are destined to rise from the ranks in which I am content to remain. Haven't you ever felt so, yourself, Harry?"

Harry's cheek flushed, and his eye lighted up.

"I won't deny that I have such thoughts sometimes," he said; "but it may end in that."

"It often does end in that; but it is only where ambition is not accompanied by faithful work. Now you are always at work. You are doing what you can to help fortune, and the end will be that fortune will help you."

"I hope so, at any rate," said Harry, thoughtfully. "I should like to fill an honorable position, and do some work by which I might be known in after years."

"Why not? The boys and young men of to-day are hereafter to fill the highest positions in the community and State. Why may not the lot fall to you?"

"I will try, at any rate, to qualify myself. Then if responsibilities come, I will try to discharge them."

The conversation was here interrupted by the entrance of Mr. Anderson, the editor of the "Gazette." He was not as well or strong as when we first made his acquaintance. Then he seemed robust enough, but now he was thinner, and moved with slower gait. It was not easy to say what had undermined his strength, for he had had no severe fit of sickness; but certainly he was in appearance several years older than when Harry entered the office.

"How do you feel this morning, Mr. Anderson?" asked Ferguson.

"I feel weak and languid, and indisposed to exertion of any kind."

"You need some change."

"That is precisely what I have thought myself. The doctor advises change of scene, and this very morning I had a letter from a brother in Wisconsin, asking me to come out and visit him."

"I have no doubt it would do you good."

"So it would. But how can I go? I can't take the paper with me," said Mr. Andersen, rather despondently.

"No; but you can leave Harry to edit it in your absence."

"Mr. Ferguson!" exclaimed Harry, startled by the proposition.

"Harry as editor!" repeated Mr. Anderson.

"Yes; why not? He is a practised writer. For more than two years he has written for two Boston papers."

"But he is so young. How old are you, Harry?" asked the editor.

"Nineteen to-day, sir."

"Nineteen. That's very young for an editor."

"Very true; but, after all, it isn't so much the age as the qualifications, is it, Mr. Anderson?"

"True," said the editor, meditatively. "Harry, do you think you could edit the paper for two or three months?"

"I think I could," said Harry, with modest confidence. His heart beat high at the thought of the important position which was likely to be opened to him; and plans of what he would do to make the paper interesting already began to be formed in his mind.

"It never occurred to me before, but I really think you could," said the editor, "and that would remove every obstacle to my going. By the way, Harry, you would have to find a new boarding-place, for Mrs. Anderson would accompany me, and we should shut up the house."

"Perhaps Ferguson would take me in?" said Harry.

"I should be glad to do so; but I don't know that my humble fare would be good enough for an editor."

Harry smiled. "I won't put on airs," he said, "till my commission is made out."

"I am afraid that I can't offer high pay for your services in that capacity," said Mr. Anderson.

"I shall charge nothing, sir," said Harry, "but thank you for the opportunity of entering, if only for a short time, a profession to which it is my ambition to belong."

After a brief consultation with his wife, Mr. Anderson appointed Harry editor pro tem., and began to make arrangements for his journey. Harry's weekly wages were raised to fifteen dollars, out of which he waa to pay Ferguson four dollars a week for board.

So our hero found himself, at nineteen, the editor of an old established paper, which, though published in a country village, was not without its share of influence in the county and State.

CHAPTER XXXII.

THE YOUNG EDITOR.

The next number of the Centreville "Gazette" contained the following notice from the pen of Mr. Anderson:—

"For the first time since our connection with the 'Gazette,' we purpose taking a brief respite from our duties. The state of our health renders a vacation desirable, and an opportune invitation from a brother at the West has been accepted. Our absence may extend to two or three months. In the interim we have committed the editorial management to Mr. Harry Walton, who has been connected with the paper, in a different capacity, for nearly three years. Though Mr. Walton is a very young man, he has already acquired a reputation, as contributor to papers of high standing in Boston, and we feel assured that our subscribers will have no reason to complain of the temporary change in the editorship."

"The old man has given you quite a handsome notice, Harry," said Ferguson.

"I hope I shall deserve it," said Harry; "but I begin now to realize that I am young to assume such responsible duties. It would have seemed more appropriate for you to undertake them."

"I can't write well enough, Harry. I like to read, but I can't produce. In regard to the business management I feel competent to advise."

"I shall certainly be guided by your advice, Ferguson."

As it may interest the reader, we will raise the curtain and show our young hero in the capacity of editor. The time is ten days after Mr. Anderson's absence. Harry was accustomed to do his work as compositor in the forenoon and the early part of the afternoon. From three to five he occupied the editorial chair, read letters, wrote paragraphs, and saw visitors. He had just seated himself, when a man entered the office and looked about him inquisitively.

"I would like to see the editor," he said.

"I am the editor," said Harry, with dignity.

The visitor looked surprised.

"You are the youngest-looking editor I have met," he said. "Have you filled the office long?"

"Not long," said Harry. "Can I do anything for you?"

"Yes, sir, you can. First let me introduce myself. I am Dr. Theophilus Peabody."

"Will you be seated, Dr. Peabody?"

"You have probably heard of me before," said the visitor.

"I can't say that I have."

"I am surprised at that," said the doctor, rather disgusted to find himself unknown. "You must have heard of Peabody's Unfailing Panacea."

"I am afraid I have not."

"You are young," said Dr. Peabody, compassionately; "that accounts for it. Peabody's Panacea, let me tell you, sir, is the great remedy of the age. It has effected more cures, relieved more pain, soothed more aching bosoms, and done more good, than any other medicine in existence."

"It must be a satisfaction to you to have conferred such a blessing on mankind," said Harry, inclined to laugh at the doctor's magniloquent style.

"It is. I consider myself one of the benefactors of mankind; but, sir, the medicine has not yet been fully introduced. There are thousands, who groan on beds of pain, who are ignorant that for the small sum of fifty cents they could be restored to health and activity."

"That's a pity."

"It is a pity, Mr. ——"

"Walton."

"Mr. Walton,—I have called, sir, to ask you to co-operate with me in making it known to the world, so far as your influence extends."

"Is your medicine a liquid?"

"No, sir; it is in the form of pills, twenty-four in a box. Let me show you."

The doctor opened a wooden box, and displayed a collection of very unwholesome-looking brown pills.

"Try one, sir; it won't do you any harm."

"Thank you; I would rather not. I don't like pills. What will they cure?"

"What won't they cure? I've got a list of fifty-nine diseases in my circular, all of which are relieved by Peabody's Panacea. They may cure more; in fact, I've been told of a consumptive patient who was considerably relieved by a single box. You won't try one?"

"I would rather not."

"Well, here is my circular, containing accounts of remarkable cures performed. Permit me to present you a box."

"Thank you," said Harry, dubiously.

"You'll probably be sick before long," said the doctor, cheerfully, "and then the pills will come handy."

"Doctor," said Ferguson, gravely, "I find my hair getting thin on top of the head. Do you think the panacea would restore it?"

"Yes," said the doctor, unexpectedly. "I had a case, in Portsmouth, of a gentleman whose head was as smooth as a billiard-ball. He took the pills for another complaint, and was surprised, in the course of three weeks, to find young hair sprouting all over the bald spot. Can't I sell you half-a-dozen boxes? You may have half a dozen for two dollars and a half."

Ferguson, who of course had been in jest, found it hard to forbear laughing, especially when Harry joined the doctor in urging him to purchase.

"Not to-day," he answered. "I can try Mr. Walton's box, and if it helps me I can order some more."

"You may not be able to get it, then," said the doctor, persuasively.
"I may not be in Centreville."
"If the panacea is well known, I can surely get it without difficulty."

"Not so cheap as I will sell it."

"I won't take any to-day," said Ferguson, decisively.

"You haven't told me what I can do for you," said Harry, who found the doctor's call rather long.

"I would like you to insert my circular to your paper. It won't take more than two columns."

"We shall be happy to insert it at regular advertising rates."

"I thought," said Dr. Peabody, disappointed, "that you might do it gratuitously, as I had given you a box."

"We don't do business on such terms," said Harry. "I think I had better return the box."

"No, keep it," said the doctor. "You will be willing to notice it, doubtless."

Harry rapidly penned this paragraph, and read it aloud:—

"Dr. Theophilus Peabody has left with us a box of his Unfailing
Panacea, which he claims will cure a large variety of diseases."
"Couldn't you give a list of the diseases?" insinuated the doctor.

"There are fifty-nine, you said?"

"Yes, sir."

"Then I am afraid we must decline."

Harry resumed his writing, and the doctor took his leave, looking far from satisfied.

"Here, Ferguson," said Harry, after the visitor had retired, "take the pills, and much good may they do you. Better take one now for the growth of your hair."

It was fortunate that Dr. Peabody did not hear the merriment that followed, or he would have given up the editorial staff of the Centreville "Gazette" as maliciously disposed to underrate his favorite medicine.

"Who wouldn't be an editor?" said Harry.

"I notice," said Ferguson, "that pill-tenders and blacking manufacturers are most liberal to the editorial profession. I only wish jewellers and piano manufacturers were as free with their manufactures. I would like a good gold watch, and I shall soon want a piano for my daughter."

"You may depend upon it, Ferguson, when such gifts come in, that I shall claim them as editorial perquisites."

"We won't quarrel about them till they come, Harry."

Our hero here opened a bulky communication.

"What is that?" asked Ferguson.

"An essay on 'The Immortality of the Soul,'—covers fifteen pages foolscap. What shall I do with it?"

"Publish it in a supplement with Dr. Peabody's circular."

"I am not sure but the circular would be more interesting reading."

"From whom does the essay come?"

"It is signed 'L. S.'"

"Then it is by Lemuel Snodgrass, a retired schoolteacher, who fancies himself a great writer."

"He'll be offended if I don't print it, won't he?"

"I'll tell you how to get over that. Say, in an editorial paragraph, 'We have received a thoughtful essay from 'L. S.', on 'The Immortality of the Soul.' We regret that its length precludes our publishing it in the 'Gazette.' We would suggest to the author to print it in a pamphlet.' That suggestion will be regarded as complimentary, and we may get the job of printing it."

"I see you are shrewd, Ferguson. I will follow your advice."

CHAPTER XXXIII.

AN UNEXPECTED PROPOSAL.

During his temporary editorship, Harry did not feel at liberty to make any decided changes in the character or arrangement of the paper; but he was ambitious to improve it, as far as he was able, in its different departments. Mr. Anderson had become rather indolent in the collection of local news, merely publishing such items as were voluntarily contributed. Harry, after his day's work was over, made a little tour of the village, gathering any news that he thought would be of interest to the public. Moreover he made arrangements to obtain news of a similar nature from neighboring villages, and the result was, that in the course of a month he made the "Gazette" much more readable.

"Really, the 'Gazette' gives a good deal more news than it used to," was a common remark.

It was probably in consequence of this improvement that new subscriptions began to come in, not from Centreville alone, but from towns in the neighborhood. This gratified and encouraged Harry, who now felt that he was on the right tack.

There was another department to which he devoted considerable attention. This was a condensed summary of news from all parts of the world, giving the preference and the largest space, of course, to American news. He aimed to supply those who did not take a daily paper with a brief record of events, such as they would not be likely, otherwise, to hear of. Of course all this work added to his labors as compositor; and his occasional sketches for Boston papers absorbed a large share of his time. Indeed, he had very little left at his disposal for rest and recreation.

"I am afraid you are working too hard, Harry," said Ferguson. "You are doing Mr. Anderson's work better than he ever did it, and your own too."

"I enjoy it," said Harry. "I work hard I know, but I feel paid by the satisfaction of finding that my labors are appreciated."

"When Mr. Anderson gets back, he will find it necessary to employ you as assistant editor, for it won't do to let the paper get back to its former dulness."

"I will accept," said Harry, "if he makes the offer. I feel more and more that I must be an editor."

"You are certainly showing yourself competent for the position."

"I have only made a beginning," said our hero, modestly. "In time I think I could make a satisfactory paper."

One day, about two months after Mr. Anderson's departure, Ferguson and Harry were surprised, and not altogether agreeably, by the entrance of John Clapp and Luke Harrison. They looked far from prosperous. In fact, both of them were decidedly seedy. Going West had not effected an improvement in their fortunes.

"Is that you, Clapp?" asked Ferguson. "Where did you come from?"

"From St. Louis."

"Then you didn't feel inclined to stay there?"

"Not I. It's a beastly place. I came near starving."

Clapp would have found any place beastly where a fair day's work was required for fair wages, and my young readers in St. Louis, therefore, need not heed his disparaging remarks.

"How was it with you, Luke?" asked Harry. "Do you like the West no better than Clapp?"

"You don't catch me out there again," said Luke. "It isn't what it's cracked up to be. We had the hardest work in getting money enough to get us back."

As Luke did not mention the kind of hard work by which the money was obtained, I may state here that an evening's luck at the faro table had supplied them with money enough to pay the fare to Boston by railway; otherwise another year might have found them still in St. Louis.

"Hard work doesn't suit your constitution, does it?" said Ferguson, slyly.

"I can work as well as anybody," said Luke; "but I haven't had the luck of some people."

"You were lucky enough to have your fare paid to the West for you."

"Yes, and when we got there, the rascal left us to shift for ourselves. That aint much luck."

"I've always had to shift for myself, and always expect to," was the reply.

"Oh, you're a model!" sneered Clapp. "You always were as sober and steady as a deacon. I wonder they didn't make you one."

"And Walton there is one of the same sort," said Luke. "I say,
Harry, it was real mean in you not to send me the money I wrote for.
You hadn't it, had you?"
"Yes," said Harry, firmly; "but I worked hard for it, and I didn't feel like giving it away."

"Who asked you to give it away? I only wanted to borrow it."

"That's the same thing—with you. You were not likely to repay it again."

"Do you mean to insult me?" blustered Luke.

"No, I never insult anybody. I only tell the truth. You know, Luke
Harrison, whether I have reason for what I say."
"I wouldn't leave a friend to suffer when I had plenty of money in my pocket," said Luke, with an injured air. "If you had been a different sort of fellow I would have asked you for five dollars to keep me along till I can get work. I've come back with empty pockets."

"I'll lend you five dollars if you need it," said Harry, who judged from Luke's appearance that he told the truth.

"Will you?" said Luke, brightening up. "That's a good fellow. I'll pay you just as soon as I can."

Harry did not place much reliance on this assurance; but he felt that he could afford the loss of five dollars, if loss it should prove, and it might prevent Luke's obtaining the money in a more questionable way.

"Where's Mr. Anderson?" asked Clapp, looking round the office.

"He's been in Michigan for a couple of months."

"You don't say so! Why, who runs the paper?"

"Ferguson and I," said Harry.

"I mean who edits it?"

"Harry does that," said his fellow-workman.

"Whew!" ejaculated Clapp, in surprise. "Why, but two years ago you was only a printer's devil!"

"He's risen from the ranks," said Ferguson, "and I can say with truth that the 'Gazette' has never been better than since it has been under his charge."

"How much does old Anderson pay you for taking his place?" asked
Luke, who was quite as much surprised as Clapp.
"I don't ask anything extra. He pays me fifteen dollars a week as compositor."

"You're doing well," said Luke, enviously. "Got a big pile of money laid up, haven't you?"

"I have something in the bank."

"Harry writes stories for the Boston papers, also," said Ferguson.
"He makes a hundred or two that way."
"Some folks are born to luck," said Clapp, discontentedly. "Here am I, six or eight years older, out of a place, and without a cent to fall back upon. I wish I was one of your lucky ones."

"You might have had a few hundred dollars, at any rate," said Ferguson, "if you hadn't chosen to spend all your money when you were earning good wages."

"A man must have a little enjoyment. We can't drudge all the time."

"It's better to do that than to be where you are now."

But Clapp was not to be convinced that he was himself to blame for his present disagreeable position. He laid the blame on fortune, like thousands of others. He could not see that Harry's good luck was the legitimate consequence of industry and frugality.

After a while the two left the office. They decided to seek their old boarding-house, and remain there for a week, waiting for something to turn up.

The next day Harry received the following letter from Mr. Anderson:—

"DEAR WALTON: My brother urges me to settle permanently at the West. I am offered a partnership in a paper in this vicinity, and my health has much improved here. The West seems the place for me. My only embarrassment is the paper. If I could dispose of the 'Gazette' for two thousand dollars cash, I could see my way clear to remove. Why can't you and Ferguson buy it? The numbers which you have sent me show that you are quite capable of filling the post of editor; and you and Ferguson can do the mechanical part. I think it will be a good chance for you. Write me at once whether there us any likelihood of your purchasing.

"Your friend,
"JOTHAM ANDERSON."

Harry's face flushed eagerly as he read this letter, Nothing would suit him better than to make this arrangement, if only he could provide the purchase money. But this was likely to present a difficulty.

CHAPTER XXXIV.

A FRIEND IN NEED.

Harry at once showed Ferguson the letter he had received.

"What are you going to do about it?" asked his friend.

"I should like to buy the paper, but I don't see how I can. Mr. Anderson wants two thousand dollars cash."
"How much have you got?"

"Only five hundred."

"I have seven hundred and fifty," said Ferguson, thoughtfully.

Harry's face brightened.

"Why can't we go into partnership?" he asked.

"That is what we spoke of once," said Ferguson, "and it would suit me perfectly; but there is a difficulty. Your money and mine added together will not be enough."

"Perhaps Mr. Anderson would take a mortgage on the establishment for the balance."

"I don't think so. He says expressly that he wants cash."

Harry looked disturbed.

"Do you think any one would lend us the money on the same terms?" he asked, after a while.

"Squire Trevor is the only man in the village likely to have money to lend. There he is in the street now. Run down, Harry, and ask him to step in a minute."

Our hero seized his hat, and did as requested. He returned immediately, followed by Squire Trevor, a stout, puffy little man, reputed shrewd and a capitalist.

"Excuse our calling you in, Squire Trevor," said Ferguson, "but we want to consult you on a matter of business. Harry, just show the squire Mr. Anderson's letter."

The squire read it deliberately.

"Do you want my advice?" he said, looking up from the perusal. "Buy the paper. It is worth what Anderson asks for it."

"So I think, but there is a difficulty. Harry and I can only raise twelve hundred dollars or so between us."

"Give a note for the balance. You'll be able to pay it off in two years, if you prosper."

"I am afraid that won't do. Mr. Anderson wants cash. Can't you lend us the money, Squire Trevor?" continued Ferguson, bluntly.

The village capitalist shook his head.

"If you had asked me last week I could have obliged you," he said; "but I was in Boston day before yesterday, and bought some railway stock which is likely to enhance in value. That leaves me short."

"Then you couldn't manage it?" said Ferguson, soberly.

"Not at present," said the squire, decidedly.

"Then we must write to Mr. Anderson, offering what we have, and a mortgage to secure the rest."

"That will be your best course."

"He may agree to our terms," said Harry, hopefully, after their visitor had left the office.

"We will hope so, at all events."

A letter was at once despatched, and in a week the answer was received.

"I am sorry," Mr. Anderson wrote, "to decline your proposals, but, I have immediate need of the whole sum which I ask for the paper. If I cannot obtain it, I shall come back to Centreville, though I would prefer to remain here."

Upon the receipt of this letter, Ferguson gave up his work for the forenoon, and made a tour of the Village, calling upon all who he thought were likely to have money to lend. He had small expectation of success, but felt that he ought to try everywhere before giving up so good a chance.

While he was absent, Harry had a welcome visitor. It was no other than Professor Henderson, the magician, in whose employ he had spent three months some years before, as related in "Bound to Rise."

"Take a seat, professor," said Harry, cordially. "I am delighted to see you."

"How you have grown, Harry!" said the professor. "Why, I should hardly have known you!"

"We haven't met since I left you to enter this office."

"No; it is nearly three years. How do you like the business?"

"Very much indeed."

"Are you doing well?"

"I receive fifteen dollars a week."

"That is good. What are your prospects for the future?"

"They would be excellent if I had a little more capital."

"I don't see how you need capital, as a journeyman printer."

"I have a chance to buy out the paper."

"But who would edit it?"

"I would."

"You!" said the magician, rather incredulously.

"I have been the editor for the last two months."

"You—a boy!"

"I am nineteen, professor."

"I shouldn't have dreamed of editing a paper at nineteen; or, indeed, as old as I am now."

Harry laughed.

"You are too modest, professor. Let me show you our last two issues."

The professor took out his glasses, and sat down, not without considerable curiosity, to read a paper edited by one who only three years before had been his assistant.

"Did you write this article?" he asked, after a pause, pointing to the leader in the last issue of the "Gazette."

"Yes, sir."

"Then, by Jove, you can write. Why, it's worthy of a man of twice your age!"

"Thank you, professor," said Harry, gratified.

"Where did you learn to write?"

Harry gave his old employer some account of his literary experiences, mentioning his connection with the two Boston weekly papers.

"You ought to be an editor," said the professor. "If you can do as much at nineteen, you have a bright future before you."

"That depends a little on circumstances. If I only could buy this paper, I would try to win reputation as well as money."

"What is your difficulty?"

"The want of money."

"How much do you need?"

"Eight hundred dollars."

"Is that all the price such a paper commands?"

"No. The price is two thousand dollars; but Ferguson and I can raise twelve hundred between us."

"Do you consider it good property?"

"Mr. Anderson made a comfortable living out of it, besides paying for office work. We should have this advantage, that we should be our own compositors."

"That would give you considerable to do, if you were editor also."

"I shouldn't mind," said Harry, "if I only had a paper of my own. I think I should be willing to work night and day."

"What are your chances of raising the sum you need?"

"Very small. Ferguson has gone out at this moment to see if he can find any one willing to lend; but we don't expect success."

"Why don't you apply to me?" asked the professor.

"I didn't know if you had the money to spare."

"I might conjure up some. Presto!—change!—you know. We professors of magic can find money anywhere."

"But you need some to work with. I have been behind the scenes," said Harry, smiling.

"But you don't know all my secrets, for all that. In sober earnest,
I haven't been practising magic these twenty-five years for nothing.
I can lend you the money you want, and I will."
Harry seized his hand, and shook it with delight.

"How can I express my gratitude?" he said.

"By sending me your paper gratis, and paying me seven per cent. interest on my money."

"Agreed. Anything more?"

"Yes. I am to give an exhibition in the village to-morrow night.
You must give me a good puff."
"With the greatest pleasure. I'll write it now."

"Before it takes place? I see you are following the example of some of the city dailies."

"And I'll print you some handbills for nothing."

"Good. When do you want the money? Will next week do?"

"Yes. Mr. Anderson won't expect the money before."

Here Ferguson entered the effice. Harry made a signal of silence to the professor, whom he introduced. Then he said:—

"Well, Ferguson, what luck?"

"None at all," answered his fellow-compositor, evidently dispirited.
"Nobody seems to have any money. We shall have to give up our plan."
"I don't mean to give it up."

"Then perhaps you'll tell me where to find the money."

"I will."

"You don't mean to say—" began Ferguson, eagerly.

"Yes, I do. I mean to say that the money is found."

"Where?"

"Prof. Henderson has agreed to let us have it."

"Is that true?" said Ferguson, bewildered.

"I believe so," said the professor, smiling. "Harry has juggled the money out of me,—you know he used to be in the business,—and you can make your bargain as soon as you like."

It is hardly necessary to say that Prof. Henderson got an excellent notice in the next number of the Centreville "Gazette;" and it is my opinion that he deserved it.

CHAPTER XXXV.

FLETCHER'S OPINION OF HARRY WALTON.

In two weeks all the business arrangements were completed, and Ferguson and Harry became joint proprietors of the "Centreville Gazette," the latter being sole editor. The change was received with favor in the village, as Harry had, as editor pro tem. for two months, shown his competence for the position. It gave him prominence also in town, and, though only nineteen, he already was classed with the minister, the doctor and the lawyer. It helped him also with the weekly papers to which he contributed in Boston, and his pay was once more raised, while his sketches were more frequently printed. Now this was all very pleasant, but it was not long before our hero found himself overburdened with work.

"What is the matter Harry? You look pale," said Ferguson, one morning.

"I have a bad headache, and am feeling out of sorts."

"I don't wonder at it. You are working too hard."

"I don't know about that."

"I do. You do nearly as much as I, as a compositor. Then you do all the editorial work, besides writing sketches for the Boston papers."

"How can I get along with less? The paper must be edited, and I shouldn't like giving up writing for the Boston papers."

"I'll tell you what to do. Take a boy and train him up as a printer. After a while he will relieve you almost wholly, while, by the time he commands good wages, we shall be able to pay them."

"It is a good idea, Ferguson. Do you know of any boy that wants to learn printing?"

"Haven't you got a younger brother?"

"The very thing," said Harry, briskly. "Father wrote to me last week that he should like to get something for ——."

"Better write and offer him a place in the office."

"I will."

The letter was written at once. An immediate answer was received, of a favorable nature. The boy was glad to leave home, and the father was pleased to have him under the charge of his older brother.

After he had become editor, and part proprietor of the "Gazette," Harry wrote to Oscar Vincent to announce his promotion. Though Oscar had been in college now nearly two years, and they seldom met, the two were as warm friends as ever, and from time to time exchanged letters.

This was Oscar's reply:—

"HARVARD COLLEGE, June 10.

"DEAR MR. EDITOR: I suppose that's the proper way to address you now. I congratulate you with all my heart on your brilliant success and rapid advancement. Here you are at nineteen, while I am only a rattle-brained sophomore. I don't mind being called that, by the way, for at least it credits me with the possession of brains. Not that I am doing so very badly. I am probably in the first third of the class, and that implies respectable scholarship here.

"But you—I can hardly realize that you, whom I knew only two or three years since as a printer's apprentice (I won't use Fletcher's word), have lifted yourself to the responsible position of sole editor. Truly you have risen from the ranks!

"Speaking of Fletcher, by the way, you know he is my classmate. He occupies an honorable position somewhere near the foot of the class, where he is likely to stay, unless he receives from the faculty leave of absence for an unlimited period. I met him yesterday, swinging his little cane, and looking as dandified as he used to.

"'Hallo! Fletcher,' said I, 'I've just got a letter from a friend of yours.'

"'Who is it?' he asked.

"'Harry Walton.'

"'He never was a friend of mine,' said Fitz, turning up his delicately chiselled nose,—'the beggarly printer's devil!'

"I hope you won't feel sensitive about the manner in which Fitz spoke of you.

"'You've made two mistakes,' said I. 'He's neither a beggar nor a printer's devil.'

"'He used to be,' retorted Fitz.

"'The last, not the first. You'll be glad to hear that he's getting on well.'

"'Has he had his wages raised twenty-five cents a week?' sneered Fitz.

"'He has lost his place,' said I.

"Fletcher actually looked happy, but I dashed his happiness by adding, 'but he's got a better one.'

"'What's that?' he snarled.

"'He has bought out the paper of Mr. Anderson, and is now sole editor and part proprietor.'

"'A boy like him buy a paper, without a cent of money and no education!'

"'You are mistaken. He had several hundred dollars, and as a writer he is considerably ahead of either of us.'

"'He'll run the paper into the ground,' said Fitz, prophetically.

"'If he does, it'll only be to give it firmer root.'

"'You are crazy about that country lout,' said Fitz. 'It isn't much to edit a little village paper like that, after all.'

"So you see what your friend Fitz thinks about it. As you may be in danger of having your vanity fed by compliments from other sources, I thought I would offset them by the candid opinion of a disinterested and impartial scholar like Fitz.

"I told my father of the step you have taken. 'Oscar,' said he, 'that boy is going to succeed. He shows the right spirit. I would have given him a place on my paper, but very likely he does better to stay where he is.'

"Perhaps you noticed the handsome notice he gave you in his paper yesterday. I really think he has a higher opinion of your talents than of mine; which, of course, shows singular lack of discrimination. However, you're my friend, and I won't make a fuss about it.

"I am cramming for the summer examinations and hot work I find it, I can tell you. This summer I am going to Niagara, and shall return by way of the St. Lawrence and Montreal, seeing the Thousand Islands, the rapids, and so on. I may send you a letter or two for the 'Gazette,' if you will give me a puff in your editorial columns."

These letters were actually written, and, being very lively and readable, Harry felt quite justified in referring to them in a complimentary way. Fletcher's depreciation of him troubled him very little.

"It will make me neither worse nor better," he reflected. "The time will come, I hope, when I shall have risen high enough to be wholly indifferent to such ill-natured sneers."

His brother arrived in due time, and was set to work as Harry himself had been three years before. He was not as smart as Harry, nor was he ever likely to rise as high; but he worked satisfactorily, and made good progress, so that in six months he was able to relieve Harry of half his labors as compositor. This, enabled him to give more time to his editorial duties. Both boarded at Ferguson's, where they had a comfortable home and good, plain fare.

Meanwhile, Harry was acknowledged by all to have improved the paper, and the most satisfactory evidence of the popular approval of his efforts came in an increased subscription list, and this, of course, made the paper more profitable. At the end of twelve months, the two partners had paid off the money borrowed from Professor Henderson, and owned the paper without incumbrance.

"A pretty good year's work, Harry," said Ferguson, cheerfully.

"Yes," said Harry; "but we'll do still better next year."

CHAPTER XXXVI.

CONCLUSION.

I have thus traced in detail the steps by which Harry Walton ascended from the condition of a poor farmer's son to the influential position of editor of a weekly newspaper. I call to mind now, however, that he is no longer a boy, and his future career will be of less interest to my young readers. Yet I hope they may be interested to hear, though not in detail, by what successive steps he rose still higher in position and influence.

Harry was approaching his twenty-first birthday when he was waited upon by a deputation of citizens from a neighboring town, inviting him to deliver a Fourth of July oration. He was at first disposed, out of modesty, to decline; but, on consultation with Ferguson, decided to accept and do his best. He was ambitious to produce a good impression, and his experience in the Debating Society gave him a moderate degree of confidence and self-reliance. When the time came he fully satisfied public expectation. I do not say that his oration was a model of eloquence, for that could not have been expected of one whose advantages had been limited, and one for whom I have never claimed extraordinary genius. But it certainly was well written and well delivered, and very creditable to the young orator. The favor with which it was received may have had something to do in influencing the people of Centreville to nominate and elect him, to the New Hampshire Legislature a few months later.

He entered that body, the youngest member in it. But his long connection with a Debating Society, and the experience he had gained in parliamentary proceedings, enabled him at once to become a useful working Member. He was successively re-elected for several years, during which he showed such practical ability that he obtained a State reputation. At twenty-eight he received a nomination for Congress, and was elected by a close vote. During all this time he remained in charge of the Centreville "Gazette," but of course had long relinquished the task of a compositor into his brother's hands. He had no foolish ideas about this work being beneath him; but he felt that he could employ his time more profitably in other ways. Under his judicious management, the "Gazette" attained a circulation and influence that it had never before reached. The income derived from it was double that which it yielded in the days of his predecessor; and both he and Ferguson were enabled to lay by a few hundred dollars every year. But Harry had never sought wealth. He was content with a comfortable support and a competence. He liked influence and the popular respect, and he was gratified by the important trusts which he received. He was ambitious, but it was a creditable and honorable ambition. He sought to promote the public welfare, and advance the public interests, both as a speaker and as a writer; and though sometimes misrepresented, the people on the whole did him justice.

A few weeks after he had taken his seat in Congress, a young man was ushered into his private room. Looking up, he saw a man of about his own age, dressed with some attempt at style, but on the whole wearing a look of faded gentility.

"Mr. Walton," said the visitor, with some hesitation.

"That is my name. Won't you take a seat?"

The visitor sat down, but appeared ill at ease. He nervously fumbled at his hat, and did not speak.

"Can I do anything for you?" asked Harry, at length.

"I see you don't know me," said the stranger.

"I can't say I recall your features; but then I see a great many persons."

"I went to school at the Prescott Academy, when you were in the office of the Centreville 'Gazette.'"

Harry looked more closely, and exclaimed, in astonished recognition,
"Fitzgerald Fletcher!"
"Yes," said the other, flushing with mortification, "I am Fitzgerald
Fletcher."
"I am glad to see you," said Harry, cordially, forgetting the old antagonism that had existed between them.

He rose and offered his hand, which Fletcher took with an air of relief, for he had felt uncertain of his reception.

"You have prospered wonderfully," said Fletcher, with a shade of envy.

"Yes," said Harry, smiling. "I was a printer's devil when you knew me; but I never meant to stay in that position. I have risen from the ranks."

"I haven't," said Fletcher, bitterly.

"Have you been unfortunate? Tell me about it, if you don't mind," said Harry, sympathetically.

"My father failed three years ago," said Fletcher, "and I found myself adrift with nothing to do, and no money to fall back upon. I have drifted about since then; but now I am out of employment. I came to you to-day to see if you will exert your influence to get me a government clerkship, even of the lowest class. You may rest assured, Mr. Walton, that I need it."

Was this the proud Fitzgerald Fletcher, suing, for the means of supporting himself, to one whom, as a boy, he had despised and looked down upon? Surely, the world is full of strange changes and mutations of fortune. Here was a chance for Harry to triumph over his old enemy; but he never thought of doing it. Instead, he was filled with sympathy for one who, unlike himself, had gone down in the social scale, and he cordially promised to see what he could do for Fletcher, and that without delay.

On inquiry, he found that Fletcher was qualified to discharge the duties of a clerk, and secured his appointment to a clerkship in the Treasury Department, on a salary of twelve hundred dollars a year. It was an income which Fletcher would once have regarded as wholly insufficient for his needs; but adversity had made him humble, and he thankfully accepted it. He holds the position still, discharging the duties satisfactorily. He is glad to claim the Hon. Harry Walton among his acquaintances, and never sneers at him now as a "printer's devil."

Oscar Vincent spent several years abroad, after graduation, acting as foreign correspondent of his father's paper. He is now his father's junior partner, and is not only respected for his ability, but a general favorite in society, on account of his sunny disposition and cordial good nature. He keeps up his intimacy with Harry Walton. Indeed, there is good reason for this, since Harry, four years since, married his sister Maud, and the two friends are brothers-in-law.

Harry's parents are still living, no longer weighed down by poverty, as when we first made their acquaintance. The legacy which came so opportunely improved their condition, and provided them with comforts to which they had long been strangers. But their chief satisfaction comes from Harry's unlooked-for success in life. Their past life of poverty and privation is all forgotten in their gratitude for this great happiness.

The next and concluding volume of this series will be

HERBERT CARTER'S LEGACY.

Note from the Editor

Odin's Library Classics strives to bring you unedited and unabridged works of classical literature. As such, this is the complete and unabridged version of the original English text unless noted. In some instances, obvious typographical errors have been corrected. This is done to preserve the original text as much as possible. The English language has evolved since the writing and some of the words appear in their original form, or at least the most commonly used form at the time. This is done to protect the original intent of the author. If at any time you are unsure of the meaning of a word, please do your research on the etymology of that word. It is important to preserve the history of the English language.

Taylor Anderson

Printed in Great Britain
by Amazon

42121612R00086